Heinemann
New Windmills

Me and My Shadow

Fifteen-year-old Emily lives a comfortable life in Edinburgh, but one day she realises that she is being followed. Who is this mysterious girl who looks so much like Emily? She is surrounded by secrets, but does Emily want to know what it is she hides?

About the Author

Joan Lingard was born in Edinburgh but grew up in Belfast. She finds inspiration for her books from the places she has lived and experienced. *Across the Barricades* was set in Northern Ireland, *Tug of War* in Latvia and *Between Two Worlds* in Canada.

She says 'Background and inheritance are very important to me in my writing. My characters are shaped by the environment they have been born into or are growing up in.'

Joan began writing when she was eleven years old and she wanted to be a novelist from that day on. She currently lives in Edinburgh, the setting for *Me and My Shadow*, with her Canadian husband. She has three children.

JOAN LINGARD

Me and My Shadow

Heinemann
New Windmills

T07816
F/LiN

Heinemann Educational Publishers
Halley Court, Jordan Hill, Oxford OX2 8EJ
A division of Harcourt Education Limited

Heinemann is a registered trademark of Harcourt Education Limited

OXFORD MELBOURNE AUCKLAND
JOHANNESBURG BLANTYRE GABORONE
IBADAN PORTSMOUTH (NH) USA CHICAGO

07 06 05 04 03
10 9 8 7 6 5 4 3 2 1

ISBN 0 435 13070 6

Cover design by Forepoint
Cover illustration by Georgios Manoli
Typeset by 🐦 Tek-Art, Croydon, Surrey

Printed and bound in the United Kingdom by Clays Ltd, St Ives plc

ME AND MY SHADOW

Me and my shadow,
Strolling down the avenue,
Me and my shadow,
Not a soul to tell one's troubles to.
And when it's twelve o'clock,
We climb the stair,
We never knock, for nobody's there,
Just me and my shadow,
All alone and feeling blue.

Billy Rose, c. 1907

Chapter 1

I first became aware of the girl on the way home from school one afternoon. Charlotte – my best friend, who I usually come home with – had a piano lesson, so I was on my own. I bypassed my street and went on down to our local shopping area at Stockbridge, where I did a little window-shopping and then went into one of the many charity shops to have a rake through the rails. My mother isn't too fond of me bringing second-hand clothes home. She says they smell and so OK, maybe they do a bit, a kind of stuffy, not-new sort of smell, but a quick wash soon sorts that out. She says we don't have to buy cast-offs, we're not that hard up.

We're not hard up at all actually. My father is a success. Don't say it like that, Emily, my mother would say if she could hear me. Like what? I'd ask innocently, knowing I'm riling her. I love my father, I really do, and I know he's a success because he's worked hard. It wasn't handed to him on a silver platter, as he's often pointed out to me. He didn't have all the privileges I'm having. It's just that he's impatient with people who are not successful. Like my older brother. Ben's not academic, he left school without too many GCSEs and now he's working with a small touring theatre company, helping to paint scenery and do odd jobs. Needless to say, he's not well paid; at times, we suspect, not paid at all. My mother gives him a backhander when he turns up, my father thinks he should come to his senses and face up to reality. What did he mean by reality? I asked him. Of course I knew he would only go on about the need to eat and have a roof over your head. I told him he had no imagination!

There wasn't much in the charity shop to tempt me that day so I didn't stay long. It was as I was coming out of the shop that I saw the girl. She was standing on the pavement with her back half turned to me. I noticed she had dark, shoulder-length hair, but that was all. I didn't really pay much attention to her at that point. The *Big Issue* seller was on the bridge as usual, and everything else looked normal. The man nodded to me as I passed. I'm a regular customer. I'd bought the current magazine from him the day before.

I crossed the road and headed up the hill to our street. It's a street of Georgian terraced houses with pretty gardens and trees overhanging the pavement. It was May and the blossom was out. I paused at our gate and glanced back along the pavement and saw the girl again, the same girl I'd seen down on the bridge. Even then I didn't think much about it. I unhooked the gate and went up the path, but as I put my key in the front door lock something made me glance round again. The girl was just passing our gate and as she did she looked straight at me and her stare sent a little shiver up my spine making my neck twitch. I gave myself a shake and went on inside thinking I was just being silly, imagining things.

The house was empty. I was used to that, coming in from school. My mother wouldn't be back from work for another hour. She's a solicitor, her speciality being family law. I dumped my backpack in the hall and ran upstairs to my bedroom, which is at the front of the house. I went to the window and looked down on the street but there was nothing to be seen, except for neat green lawns and flowering cherry trees and rose bushes and empty parked cars. Parked cars are the curse of the street but there are no garages since in Georgian times there was no need for them. They kept their coaches elsewhere and had them brought round when they were needed.

Why had the girl given me the shivers? Why had she been staring at me? She had nothing to do with me, after all, nothing that I could see. Maybe she just resented me living in a 'posh' street, wearing the uniform of a 'posh' girls' school. Maybe she herself was homeless. I hadn't noticed how she was dressed exactly, but I thought she might have been wearing jeans and a black top. I went back downstairs and made myself a cup of coffee and a sandwich and sat at the kitchen table to eat it. I opened a magazine, but I didn't read it. I couldn't get the girl out of my head. I felt as if I should have recognised her, that I had seen her or met her somewhere before, but I couldn't think where.

I was still puzzling over this when I heard the front door opening and Ben's voice calling, 'Anybody in?'

I ran to meet him and forgot all about the girl. We bear-hugged and I asked him how long he was home for and he said only for the night. Wasn't he going to be able to stay till Saturday then? Mum and Dad would be disappointed if he didn't. They were having a party to celebrate their silver wedding anniversary, not that either Ben or I thought that was something terribly special, being married twenty-five years, but of course our parents did. Ben said it was out of the question for him to stay; they had just come into Edinburgh for the day to sort out their props and tomorrow would set off touring up in the north-west – Mallaig and Ullapool, places like that. I wished I could go with them and he said I'd better put ideas like that out of my head, they wouldn't be popular, not in this house.

'You've got the brains, girl! You're the academic hope of the family, don't forget that!'

I didn't want to be the hope of anybody other than myself. Not that I knew exactly what I did hope for myself. I changed my mind every other day.

'I'd like to travel. Even if it's only up north. Or go on the stage!' I added airily, though I did, in fact, quite fancy that. It was an ambition that I had previously only voiced to Charlotte, who had done her best to put me off. A second cousin twice removed of her mother's had made that ghastly mistake, had spent her life playing bit parts in between long spells of 'resting', and for her pains was forced now to live in a damp basement eating past-the-sell-by-date food. Charlotte is full of such cautionary tales, fed to her by her mother, I guess.

'Fifteen's a bad age.' Ben grinned at me. 'It's a restless age.'

He should know. He had been very restless from fifteen through to seventeen and there had been ongoing rows in the house about his late nights and the kind of friends he hung out with. All normal teenage stuff, our mother had commented wryly, thinking that by eighteen he would have come to his senses and started to study so that he would have the chance of a university place, even if it was to one of the 'minor' universities (as she describes them) that had once been polytechnics and further education colleges.

We sat at the table drinking coffee and Ben told me all about the play they were doing, a two-hander between a drug addict who has just discovered he is HIV positive and a former girlfriend who is naturally worried that she might be also. It was quite 'gritty', he said. And 'meaty'. Most of their plays were loaded with meat and grit, and the number of characters had to be limited on account of lack of funds. 'Sounds like a laugh a minute,' our father had said after hearing about one play. I had seen it myself and come home feeling depressed, though I didn't tell Ben that. He was into 'the darker side of life', though to look at him you'd never imagine it. He's blond and blue-eyed, like our mother, and when he was younger he had a cherubic look to him, unlike me, who's always been thin and dark. Like my father. Yes, I look very much like my father.

When our mother came in she was delighted to see Ben. He brings a ray of sunshine into our house. I saw her after-work tiredness ebbing away at the sight of him. 'You should come home more often!' He had jumped up to give her a hug and now he was standing with his arm round her shoulder smiling.

'I come home as often as I can, Mum.'

She wanted him to come back permanently to Edinburgh, and lead a more settled life. Not get married, of course, not that. He was only twenty. But she worried that he didn't eat properly, that he didn't get enough sleep, that he drank too much, that he might be into drugs, that the rest of the company might be a bad influence on him. All typical mother stuff.

When our father came in an hour later he was also pleased to see Ben. Although he disapproves of Ben's lifestyle and they don't agree about much, they've never fallen out seriously. So you see, we were a fairly united family. *Were*.

We had a good evening all together, the four of us, the only blip being when Ben told Dad he wouldn't be here for their party. That didn't go down well.

'Don't you think you should make the effort, Ben?'

'Dad, it's not a case of making an effort. It's my job.'

'Job!' Dad humphed.

'But it is. They need me there. I can't let them down.'

'But you can let us down?'

'They're relying on me being there.'

'The show must go on,' I put in unhelpfully.

'We'll just have to have the family celebration tonight,' said our mother, who is good at lowering the temperature.

'Oh, all right,' our father sighed.

He recovered his spirits and brought out a couple of what he called 'decent' bottles of red wine from his cellar for dinner and didn't even remark, as he tended to do, when he refilled my glass, that I shouldn't be drinking so much. He was relaxed now. He told us he'd made a good deal that day. When I said he was always making good deals he only laughed. He's an estate agent and a property developer and has various other interests, whatever that means. I had never been interested enough to find out. He asked Ben about the theatre group in a good-natured way and seemed genuinely entertained by some of the misfortunes that befell it. Ben is an amusing teller of tales. His group is always arriving at village halls in the back of beyond to find there's been a power cut and they've got no lighting or heating, or that there are only ten chairs for an audience of twenty, or that the house consists of one man who has bought a ticket and insists on having the whole performance played to him from beginning to end with even the offer of his money back and a lift home not moving him. As you might guess, their shows are seldom big sell-outs, and that's why our father thinks they're just 'playing' at theatres, the way we used to do with our friends in the back garden, raising money for charities like the Red Cross and the Lifeboats. Ben had always been the star of the show. I was surprised that he himself hadn't gone into acting.

In the middle of the meal the phone rang and Dad said, 'Drat that thing! Why does it always have to ring when we're eating?' I hurried to get it. It would probably be for me anyway, my mother said as I left the table. I thought it might be Charlotte. We ring each other for a blether most evenings. My mother says she doesn't know what we can find to talk about when we've parted only a short time before.

I lifted the receiver and said hello. There was silence at the other end but not a dead silence. I said hello again and waited, ignoring my mother's advice about putting the receiver down straight away if you get an odd phone call. I sensed that there was someone at the other end, also waiting. It wasn't *deep* breathing exactly, but I could hear that the caller was still there. Then came a click as he – or she – disconnected. I went back to the table.

'Who was it?' asked my mother.

'Wrong number.'

The phone rang again ten minutes later.

'You go this time, Ben,' I said.

He went and returned a minute later. He shrugged. 'They put the receiver down. Must have been another wrong number. Or the same one.'

It didn't ring again.

Ben was still in bed when I left for school in the morning. He's used to going to bed late, getting up late. That's showbiz for you! That's what he says. I put my head round his door and said to the heap under the downie, 'See you later, Big Brother! Come home for longer next time!'

His head shot up like a jack-in-the-box, his hair all tousled. He blinked at me.

'And remember to phone on Saturday night and wish Mum and Dad a happy anniversary.'

'Sure thing. Take care, Kiddo!'

'Kiddo yourself!' I made a face at him and left him to his slumbers. He'd be gone by the time I came home from school. I missed him in the house. The place seemed so quiet without him leaping about and playing his music and he'd always had lots of friends around. Mum encourages us to bring our friends home. I know she'd rather know who we're hanging out with. I suppose it makes her feel she's still in control, at least partially.

Dad ran me to school, picking up Charlotte on the way. She'd had a date the night before with a boy she'd just met who had sounded promising, and I was dying to hear about it, but she waited until we were out of the car before she told me anything.

'He was a right drip,' she declared, as soon as we'd slammed the car doors behind us. 'He talked about *golf* all evening, would you believe it!'

So that was the end of that. If there is anything Charlotte hates it's golf. Both her parents are golf fanatics and can't understand why their daughter hasn't taken to the game in spite of the fact that they bought her a set of junior clubs when she was seven and dragged her round a number of windy courses until one day she rebelled and sat down in the middle of a bunker and refused to move until they promised to take her home. She's stubborn is my best friend. (She says I am too.) And she's certainly not overly fond of outdoor sports.

We had a normal day at school and afterwards Charlotte and I walked home together – it's quite a way but it gives us plenty of time for a gossip and sometimes we meet up with a couple of boys on their way home, which happened that afternoon. We were chatting and laughing and then I happened to look round.

On the pavement, about twenty metres behind us, was the girl. I definitely saw her.

'Charlotte,' I said in a low voice, 'there's a girl following us.'

'What?' Charlotte looked round and so did I, and then the boys did too. The pavement was empty. 'There's nobody there, Emmie. You must have been seeing things! What would a girl be doing following us?'

'She might be after Donald and me,' suggested Mark.

'You should be so lucky!' said Charlotte.

We ended up going for coffee with the boys. In the cafe I was sitting facing the street; the others had their backs to it. When I saw the girl passing the door, somehow or other I was not surprised and I said nothing to Charlotte or the boys. The girl looked in and met my eye and once more I felt that little shiver of unease. Was she stalking me? If so, why? Or was she just a figment of my imagination?

Chapter 2

If she *was* a figment of my imagination I must be going loopy. I gave my cappuccino a vigorous stir and stared into the swirling froth. The boys were asking if we'd like a game of tennis that evening.

Mark gave me a nudge. 'What's up with you? You look spaced out.'

'Tennis?' Charlotte was groaning. No doubt she would rather go to the cinema or spend the evening in a variety of coffee establishments, of which there is no lack in the city. Every time a shop becomes vacant a new coffee bar moves in. I fancied a game of tennis though, I felt like doing something physical instead of sitting drinking cappuccinos until I was coffee-logged. Whacking a ball round a court sounded attractive.

'Count me in,' I said.

'And me out,' said Charlotte.

'Come on, Charlie, don't be such a lazy loon. You need the exercise. Half the country's teenagers are obese.'

'Are you calling me obese?'

'I said *half* the teenagers. Do you think I'd dare call you obese?'

She made a face at me.

'So what about a game?' put in Donald.

'Fine by me,' I said.

'It's all right for you, you can hit the stupid ball,' mumped Charlotte.

And I hit it pretty hard that evening. It was as if I was full of pent-up energy. Mark and I wiped the floor – or the damp ground, rather, for it had been raining – with

Donald and Charlotte (for of course she did come and I had known that she would since she doesn't like to be left out of anything), and then when I partnered Charlotte, in spite of having her as a handicap (as I told her), we almost beat the boys. I was about to deliver a blistering return which would have more or less wrapped up the game for us when I glanced over at the road and saw my shadow standing there. I muffed the shot and from then on was off my stroke.

I was off my stroke in school the next day as well. I couldn't concentrate and several times lost the thread of what was going on. Between classes I gravitated over to the classroom window to see if she might be out there too. And just before lunch, she was! The next time I looked, though, she was gone.

After school I was even more on tenterhooks. When I turned a corner I surveyed the street ahead of me before moving on and I kept glancing over my shoulder. Everywhere I went I felt as if someone was watching me.

'What's up with you today?' asked Charlotte. 'You're all twitchy.'

'You remember I thought a girl was following us?'

'You're not on that again! What have you been taking, Emmie?'

'Caffeine. I'm thinking of kicking the habit.'

'But what would a girl want to follow you for?'

'But, seriously, I *have* seen a girl, Charlie, honestly I have. She's about my height and she's got dark hair, straight, down to her shoulders –'

'Sure you haven't been looking in the mirror?'

'You don't believe me, do you? If I see her today I'll tell you straight away, OK?'

'OK.'

We went down to Stockbridge and did a trawl along the charity shops with me keeping an extra-sharp lookout.

Charlotte tried something on in nearly every shop, she's a compulsive trier-on, and so was in a cubicle with one leg inside a pair of jeans when I sighted the girl.

'Quick, Charlie! I've seen her!'

'I can't come out like this.'

By the time she'd hauled the jeans up over her hips and followed me to the door the girl had vanished and the woman in charge of the shop thought we were about to make a run for it without paying. We explained that we'd thought we'd seen a friend in the street.

'So, do you wish to take the jeans?' asked the woman, her eagle eye fixed firmly on us.

But the trousers, being only size eight, wouldn't meet round Charlotte's waist even though she took a deep breath and sucked in her stomach. 'I think I'll need to go on a diet,' she announced, eyeing herself in the mirror. She was always going on a diet, and coming off. She said it was OK for me, I was rail-thin and could eat anything, and did. Gutsy Malone, she called me.

Back in the street, there was no sign of my stalker.

'Are you certain you've not been taking anything, Emmie? Maybe it *is* too many cappuccinos!'

I wished the reason could be as simple. Easy enough to drink less coffee but not, it seemed, to get rid of my stalker. It was a horrible word, 'stalker'. It brought to mind some of the nasty cases that had been in the paper. Celebrities seemed to have dozens after them. Not that I was a celebrity, or not that I knew of.

On Saturday morning we were busy with preparations for the party. My mother had everything pretty well organised, she always does, so it was just a case of moving the furniture around in the drawing room and letting in the caterers and the woman who was arranging the flowers. Mum and I both went to the hairdresser's, at her insistence, and the one who did me wanted to cut my hair, but I decided against it. Although, as I sat there contemplating myself in the mirror, I wondered if perhaps I should get it cut really short, for then the girl might not recognise me. This was getting ridiculous! She might not even exist. I was beginning to think that I really had been hallucinating.

'What are you frowning for, Emily?' asked my mother, who was sitting in the chair next to mine, wrapped up in a similar black-cloak affair. 'You'll be left with a ridge between your eyebrows if you go on like that.'

Her remark only made me frown all the more.

'I just want the ends trimmed,' I told my hairdresser. 'No more than half an inch off.'

Coming out of the hairdresser's I scanned the street, but there was no sign of my shadow. Maybe she'd disappeared into the haar, the Edinburgh mist that creeps in off the North Sea.

'What's got into you this last couple of days?' asked my mother. 'Anything troubling you, dear? You know you must tell me if there is.'

'No, nothing.' I shook my head and avoided her eye.

We went home then, my mother and I.

At eight o'clock the guests began to arrive. Charlotte's mother and father were amongst them; they are very old friends of my parents and had been at each other's weddings. Charlotte had been invited as well so that I would have someone of my own age to keep me company. The two of us were expected to pass things round, along with the couple of waitresses from the catering firm. We didn't mind that; in fact, we rather enjoyed it. I smiled blithely at the various comments I received. *My goodness, Emily, how you've grown! I wouldn't have known you! Quite the young lady, aren't you? You must be as tall as your mother, perhaps even taller? You're so like your father, Emily!*

He loves a party and was in a very good mood, smiling hugely and every now and then he would throw a fond look at my mother and she would return it.

'Do you think they can still be in love?' asked Charlotte wistfully.

She was going through a romantic stage and was in love with the idea of being in love. She hadn't yet found anyone to fit the picture, though she was rather sweet on my brother, Ben, who, at the moment, she conceded, was too old for her. Or rather, she was too young for him. She had declared she was going to go all out for him when she was seventeen, for then the gap of five years wouldn't matter so much. I had very mixed feelings about the idea of Charlotte 'getting' him, but I didn't think she had much chance as he currently had a girl in the theatre company who was twenty-four and 'streetwise'. That was how my mother had summed up Posy when Ben had brought her home. The visit had not been an overwhelming success. My mother had disliked the battery of rings piercing Posy's ears and nose and the fact that everything possible about her was black from the tips of her short spiky hair down to the blunt toes of her Doc Martens. She wore black eyeshadow, black lipstick, black polish on her fingernails and no doubt on her toenails, too, as my mother remarked wryly. After she'd gone, of course. My father said in that get-up she should be leading one of the ghost tours for tourists on the Royal Mile. (They are pretty conservative in their tastes, my parents. I quite liked her. She gave me a bottle of her black nail polish.) My father also said he found it difficult to believe that anyone had actually been named Posy on a birth certificate, though apparently she had.

'I suppose they could still be in love,' I said to Charlotte.

My parents' relationship had always been a romantic one. They celebrated every anniversary in style, including the one of the day that they'd first met, and Dad often bought flowers for Mum. I took another swig of fizz. Charlotte and I had glasses parked behind the potted plant in the hall and in between ferrying plates of nibbles around we returned there to refresh ourselves.

By now the party was in full swing. Most of the guests had arrived and from the drawing room came the sound of raised voices and laughter and the clink of glasses. We decided we could lie low for a bit, down in the hall. We had to listen for the doorbell anyway. No one in the drawing room would have a hope in hell of hearing anything, possibly not even one another. The noise level was fairly high.

I swiped another bottle from the table in the hall and recharged our glasses. The doorbell rang and just as I was going to answer it the telephone joined in.

'Will I get it?' asked Charlotte, indicating the phone.

'Yes, do that!' I opened the door to Mr and Mrs Watson, who hadn't seen me for some time and were astonished by how grown up I was!

'You must be as tall as your mother now, Emily.'

'Taller! I can see over the top of her head.' If I had another glass of wine I felt I would be flying. 'Do come in, Mr and Mrs Watson!' I said with a flourish.

Mrs Watson gave me an uneasy little smile. I took their coats and ushered them upstairs into the drawing room. Charlotte was in the doorway, standing on tiptoe.

'I'm looking for your dad,' she said. 'The phone call is for him.'

'I'll find him.' I worked my way into the crowd until I saw him standing by the fireplace. He had one arm resting on it and he was chatting amiably. 'Dad!' I yelled. 'Phone!'

He frowned for a moment, then nodded and excused himself. He followed me out of the room. 'You didn't have to shout!'

14

'You wouldn't have heard me in the middle of that din unless I did.'

The receiver was lying beside the phone on the hall table. He lifted it and said, 'John Malone speaking.'

He listened and his face blanched, it really did, I saw it. It took on a kind of pallid white behind the tan he'd acquired when he and my mother went skiing in the Alps at Easter.

'Just a moment, I'll take the call in my study.' To me he said, 'Put the receiver down, Emily, would you, please, once I get into my study.'

I took it from his hand and held it a little away from my body as if it was contaminated. Then I put it to my ear and listened. I could hear background noises, voices and laughter, a bit like what was going on in our drawing room only not so hectic. It sounded like someone was phoning from a cafe or a pub. Then came my father's voice saying, 'All right, Emily, you can put the phone down now.'

I didn't dare not do it, even though I was sorely tempted not to. But he would have listened for the click before saying anything else.

Charlotte came out of the kitchen eating a chicken vol-au-vent.

'Who was it on the phone?' I asked her. 'Was it a man?'

She shook her head and when she'd finished eating said, 'A girl.'

'A *girl*?' It couldn't be *her*, surely? Though I had a sinking feeling in the pit of my stomach that it might be. She was bad news, whoever she was, and whatever she was up to. What *could* she be up to? 'Not an older woman?'

'She sounded young. Well, about our age, I would say.'

'What was her voice like? Did she have an accent?'

'London, I think. Sort of twangy. I mean, she didn't say much, only, "Can I speak to Mr John Malone, please?"'

'Didn't you ask who was calling?'

'I never thought to. What's up, anyway?'

'I don't know.' I had sobered up pretty quickly and the thought of any more fizzy wine made me feel sick.

We hovered in the hall until my father reappeared from his study. He had been on the phone for all of twenty minutes. His face looked drawn and his *joie de vivre* had fled.

'Are you all right, Dad?' I asked.

'Fine, fine.' He passed a hand over his forehead, which shone as if damp.

'Who was it on the phone?'

'No one. No one you know. I'd better go back in.'

I went in after him and watched him carefully. I was petrified in case he'd had some kind of shock and might keel over with a heart attack. He was fifty-five after all and he worked too hard. My mother was always telling him so. She also was watching him and looking puzzled at the change that had come over him though he was doing his best to remain the jovial host. I think we were all glad when the last guest left and we could close the front door behind them.

'Are you all right, John?' asked my mother.

'Just tired, dear. A good night's sleep . . .'

He climbed the stairs wearily, like an old man, holding on to the banister rail whereas normally he liked to run up and down. His little effort to keep fit, he would joke.

I had the feeling that whatever trouble the phone call had stirred up, it would not vanish with a good night's sleep.

Chapter 3

At breakfast, my father, who was eating virtually nothing, said, 'I'm afraid I must go into the office for a little while this morning, Mary.'

'Must you?' My mother looked dismayed. 'It's Sunday! Don't you think you could give the place a miss for one day? We talked about going down the coast, remember, having lunch somewhere?'

'I won't be long,' he promised, and rose from the table. 'I'll be back in time to take you for lunch.' And with that he was gone.

'I wish he wouldn't work so hard,' said my mother for about the millionth time. We all wished he wouldn't. Ben had sworn that he wasn't going to get on a treadmill and be a slave to a machine the way our father was. I sometimes wonder if that was why he had gone off in a totally different direction. My mother sighed. She worked hard herself but knew when to take time off. She is a very well-balanced person. Everyone who knows her would say so.

I got up and carried my mug and plate over to the dishwasher.

'What are you planning to do today, Emily?'

'I thought I might go for a ride on my bike. It seems quite a nice day. Sun's out.'

'Just be careful.' She doesn't like me cycling round the city.

'The traffic's not so bad on Sunday,' I said to mollify her.

'Wear your helmet.'

'I will.'

'Are you seeing Charlotte?'

'Probably.' I was in a hurry to escape now. 'See you later!'

I took my helmet from the hall cupboard and rammed it on my head. Then I quickly lifted my bike out of the front porch (my mother hates it being there, cluttering the place up) and wheeled it down the path. I didn't look back in case she would come out and ask me some more questions.

The traffic was light. It was only ten o'clock, which is early for a Sunday morning. A few people were about, carrying bundles of newspapers under their arms. In no time at all I was cutting through Stockbridge and heading for Leith and the docks.

It was quiet down here too. Some cafes were opening their doors. The grey ship, moored near the bridge, once a 'floating restaurant', looked sad and neglected. You couldn't say the same for the *Britannia*, which is berthed in an outer part of the port. My father took me to see the ship for a birthday treat. It's open to the public, at a price. We had lunch afterwards at a restaurant on the water's edge.

The office he runs his property business from is in an old converted warehouse, not far from the docks. A lot of the old property has been converted into smart flats and trendy restaurants. He grew up down here, long before the place was 'tarted up', as he calls it. His family was poor. They lived in an old tenement flat with a shared loo on the stairs. His dad was a semi-invalid and out of work most of the time and his mother cleaned tenement stairs to support the family. So you can see how well my dad has done for himself.

I approached his office building cautiously, slackening off on the pedals. I reckoned he must be there by this time and he was. His car was parked nearby. I wheeled my bike round the corner and propped it against the wall, where it would be out of sight. I took off my helmet and laid it on the seat. My father's office is at the back of the building, so the chances were that he wouldn't be able to see me or my bike. I had no idea what I was going to do, or exactly why I had come. I had acted impulsively, something I'm prone to do. My mother tells me I should pause to think, it only takes a minute but it can save hours of anguish. She's probably right.

I hovered on the corner, keeping the door of the building under surveillance. Five minutes or so later, it opened and out came my father. He didn't make for his car, as I might have expected him to do. He went past it and began to walk in the direction of the river. He was walking with his head down as if anxious not to see or be seen by anyone. Usually he walks with his head up, his shoulders back, and steps out briskly like a man who knows where he's going and doesn't want to waste any time. Yet again I didn't stop to think, I set off in pursuit. He didn't look round once. I followed him in fits and starts, taking refuge in alleys or doorways whenever I could. It was only when he was about to cross the bridge over the river that I remembered my bike! But I couldn't go back to lock it up now, I'd lose him if I did.

Halfway across the bridge he paused to look over the water. Maybe that was all he had come out for: a bit of a break, a breath of sea air. I pulled back, kept my own head down. I stared into the dark, oily water. At the edge lay a frill of scum. People's discards. Bits of plastic. Old boxes. Pizza lids. A trio of ducks swimming in v-formation glided smoothly past and disappeared under the bridge. But all the time I had one eye on the man on the bridge.

He straightened up suddenly and pushed his hair back from his face. I had the feeling that he sighed, though of course I couldn't have heard it. Was he going to come back this same way and return to his office? But he didn't, he carried on and crossed the short stretch of bridge to the other side. I waited a moment, then went after him. He turned right into a street where there are a number of cafes and restaurants. I was just in time to see him disappearing into one on the corner.

On the opposite side of the road a fat pillar offered fairly good cover, and there was a telephone box close by that I could dive into if necessary. The cafe had three entrances and lots of windows. My father didn't appear to be sitting anywhere near a window, however, not as far as I could make out. I did feel a bit guilty to be spying on him like this, but I hastily pushed that quibble out of the way. I had to. I had to find out what was going on.

Ten minutes went by before the rain started. I had come out in T-shirt and jeans. I dived into the telephone box and lifted the receiver to make it look as if I were making a call. I'd hardly been there for more than a minute when a woman with an umbrella came and stood outside, eyeing me stonily through the glass. I turned my back, but eventually I had to surrender the box to her.

The rain was showing no sign of letting up. I was soon damp and shivery and beginning to wonder if Dad's movements were connected in any way to last night's mysterious phone call. It might be true that he'd had some work at the office to attend to and had come out simply to have coffee and a croissant to compensate for the little he'd eaten at breakfast. Was there a simple explanation to everything that was happening? Was it complex only in my head? Had I become too suspicious? The girl who'd been following me might just be a bit of an oddball. But why had she picked me to stalk? My head was confused. I couldn't seem to make sense of anything.

I looked at my watch. He had been in the cafe for twenty-five minutes so far, which seemed a long time to take having a cup of coffee. If you were on your own, that is. *Was* he on his own?

I massaged the goose pimples on my arms. How much longer could I hang on here? I was debating this when I saw my father emerge from the cafe. I shrank back behind the pillar. He crossed the road and passed quite close to me, but his shoulders were hunched and his head was lowered against the rain so he didn't see me. I was grateful now for the downpour. I let out my breath in a long, relieved sigh. I'd give him five minutes and then make a dash for it.

So concerned was I in watching him that I almost missed the girl coming out of the cafe. She was wearing an anorak with the hood pulled up covering her hair and part of her face but there was no question but that it was her. I felt I would know her anywhere. She was running as if to get out of the rain. Before I could get geared up she had reached the corner and disappeared round it. I shot after her, reversing our former roles. For a change, I would be the one to call the shots. I would follow *her*.

But when I rounded the corner, she had gone! I couldn't believe it. Now you see her, now you don't. It was at moments like that that I seriously began to wonder if I was going off my trolley. Surely she couldn't have disappeared, *just* like that? It seemed, though, that she had. She could have gone into a shop or a doorway. I searched up and down the street for the next twenty minutes or so, feeling more and more frustrated. She must have seen me and deliberately 'lost' me.

I gave up and made my way back to my father's office. His car was gone. And then when I went round the corner to fetch my bike I found that it had gone too. *Oh no!* I wanted to sit down on the ground and drum my heels. Have a tantrum. There was I, shivering in damp clothes, without one penny in my pocket. I could have rung home and reversed the charges, but what was I to say to them?

I was pondering what to do next when a voice behind me said, 'Is that you, Emily?'

I turned to see my father's unmarried sister, my Aunt Etta, facing me.

'What are you doing down here, love? Goodness, you're wet! Looking for your dad, are you?'

'No, not exactly,' I said awkwardly. 'I just came out for a run on my bike.'

I felt awkward on more than one count. It was partly that I was afraid she might tell Dad I'd been there and the other part was that we don't see her very often as she and my mother don't get on. My mother has tried, I do believe she has, but Aunt Etta keeps making remarks that annoy her when she comes to visit, commenting on the price of our furniture and so forth. 'That settee must have cost a quid or two.' 'Off to Italy again, are you?' She's a dinner lady at a local primary school and my father helps her out financially. He usually visits her on his own and sometimes I go with him and when I do she's quite different, much nicer. We usually have a good time. She tells us stories about the school dinner service and makes us laugh. My mother and she just seem to rub each other up the wrong way.

'I'd better go and collect my bike,' I said, trying to edge away.

'I hope you've left it locked up. They're always being nicked round here.'

'Same with us.'

'Well, you'd expect that, wouldn't you? I mean, in a district like yours.'

I gave her a half-smile.

'You'll need to come and see me soon with your dad. It's been a while.'

'I will,' I promised.

'I like you coming, you know. Come for your tea one day.'

I made my escape and set off to walk the three miles home. On the way another shower swept over the city, thoroughly drenching me this time.

* * *

When I did make it home I found that my parents had gone out, and I had no key. I went round to Charlotte's. They were in, thank goodness for that at least! I'd been thinking I might be out of luck with everything today. Charlotte's mother fussed over my sopping clothes and said I must have a shower immediately before I caught my death and Charlotte would find me some dry clothes, which was not all that easy since I am three inches taller than her. I ended up in a skimpy sweatshirt and jeans that stopped three inches above my ankles. Mrs McDowell offered to lend me something out of her wardrobe but I declined, with thanks, since she is very large and fond of polyester.

'What on earth were you doing?' demanded Charlotte once I was showered and clean and dry and we were sitting on her bed drinking hot chocolate and eating chocolate biscuits, which Charlotte had sworn off the day before.

I told her I'd gone down to Leith and parked my bike in the street and someone had stolen it. It was only six months old and had cost what my father called 'a packet'. When he was a boy he'd had second-hand bikes that had been bought for next to nothing.

'You'd better report it to the police, hadn't you? Otherwise you won't be able to claim on the insurance.'

Charlotte's father works for an insurance company so she is up on these things. She told him about my stolen bike when we were having lunch – her mother asked me to stay – and he wanted to report it for me then and there.

'It's all right,' I protested. 'I don't want to bother you.'

'No bother, Emily.' He was up out of his seat and reaching for a pad and paper. 'Where did you leave it?'

'Down at Leith.' Charlotte spoke for me, though I had not intended to tell that to my own parents. I was going to have made up a location. Outside the Botanic Garden.

Something like that. What do they say about once you first practise to deceive . . .? I can't remember the ending of it, but I'm not sure it's not good.

'At Leith?' Charlotte's mother frowned. 'Do you mean at the docks?'

'Not quite down at Leith.' I had to cough, I was choking on my bread roll. 'It's all right, honestly. I'm sure Dad would rather sort it out himself.'

'Very well.' Charlotte's father sat down again.

After lunch, Charlotte and I went out, on foot since I was bikeless. I wasn't keen on being seen in public in sawn-off jeans, but I had no choice. I was less keen on being pumped further by Charlotte's parents. I'd have my own to face later. *You're so careless, Emily! You ought to look after your things better. Money doesn't grow on trees, you know. We have to work for it* . . . I could have written the script myself and saved them the effort of saying it all.

The sun had come out again. We headed up town, to Princes Street, and did a tour of the shops; then we crossed the road. On the space at the side of the art galleries a lot of people were hanging around. There's often something going on there. Groups playing, jugglers juggling, preachers preaching. Today, a Peruvian group was performing. They were lively and good fun and the crowd was enjoying the music. We listened for a while before drifting on. We made for the Playfair Steps, which take you up the hill towards the Old Town.

A man and a girl, wrapped in pieces of old grey blanket, were sitting at the foot of the steps. There was nothing unusual in that. It was a favourite spot for beggars. A fierce-looking dog kept guard at their side, its tongue lolling between large yellow teeth. In front of them a card was propped, a card saying 'HUNGRY AND HOMELESS' and a hat into which a few coins, a very few, had been tossed.

'Spare something for a cup of hot tea, young ladies,' the man called out.

I had no money on me so was relieved of the need to decide whether to give them anything or not. I always feel guilty when I pass anyone who claims to be homeless although I know that my father is probably right when he says that much of it is a scam. Vans are supposed to drop beggars off in the city in the mornings and collect them when they've done their day's stint. The *Big Issue* sellers are in a different category. Charlotte, who had some money on her, though not much, enough for a couple of cups of coffee, looked straight ahead and pretended not to hear. I couldn't help glancing sideways, that's one of the habits that lands me in trouble, I'm too nosy to walk on. And I looked straight into the eyes of the girl. *My* girl.

Chapter 4

I stopped dead in front of her.

'I know you,' I said.

'Do you?' She didn't blink, she had a very steady stare. I realised that I was trembling although I wasn't sure why I should be. Why should she trouble me so much?

Charlotte had halted two steps up and was frowning down at me. 'Emily,' she called, 'come on!'

Her voice broke my trance. I dropped my gaze and turned and went to rejoin her.

'It's a mistake to start talking to them,' said Charlotte, sounding very like her mother. 'They're probably on drugs. You never know what they might do. They could turn the dog loose or anything.'

She knew I was afraid of dogs, I'd been chased by one when I was younger, and bitten on the ankle. It had only been a terrier, but its bite was nasty enough and I'd had to have an anti-tetanus jab straight away. Fortunately it didn't have rabies! Since then I'd given dogs a wide berth.

I didn't tell Charlotte that the girl sitting on the ground wrapped in a blanket was the one who had been following me. She was to be my secret now, mine and my father's, though it was not one that we were sharing together.

He was not pleased when he came to hear the tale of my lost bike. It was the second that I'd lost in a year.

'Did you imagine that if you left it unpadlocked outside the Botanics on a Sunday morning that it would be there when you got back? For someone who's supposed to be intelligent you can behave amazingly stupidly at times,

Emily. Well, you can just jolly well do without a bike for a while!'

He would relent before long, he always does, for although he can be hot-tempered he doesn't hold a grudge. My mother never loses her temper, but she doesn't forgive quite so quickly. I find her disapproval worse and I hate it when she's disappointed in me, as does Ben. But he says he can't lead his life just to please our mother, nor would she ask him to, not openly. She has high standards, and growing up we have always been aware of them. I slid out of the drawing room and went upstairs. I didn't really care if I got another bike or not. I was too preoccupied with other things.

My father reported the loss of the bike, giving the serial number and so forth to the police, though we knew that it was unlikely to be recovered. Bikes went missing all the time and the police had more to do than go chasing after them. Half of them were nicked for resale anyway and whisked off into garages to be taken apart and reassembled. We were therefore very surprised to get a call later saying that it had been found.

'Where was it?' asked my father. 'Down at Leith, you say? Where exactly? Yes, I do know that part. It's just opposite my office, as a matter of fact. Quite a coincidence, eh?'

I put my hands over my cheeks in an effort to cool them down. Talk about being consumed with guilt! I felt as if a fiery furnace was yawning at my feet, ready to burn me to a frazzle. But it was good news that the bike had turned up. Someone must merely have borrowed it and put it back in the same spot afterwards.

My father replaced the receiver. 'You've been lucky, madam. Not that you deserve it!'

'No,' I agreed.

'Odd that it should be found so close to your office,' said my mother thoughtfully.

'Odd that the police should have found anything!' he rejoined.

I was glad that it was left at that. I went to the police station to collect it. Everything was intact. Even the helmet was there.

Charlotte was preparing for her Grade Six piano exam (she wants to do music when she leaves school, though her parents would rather she did law or medicine, leading the way to a reliable, well-paid career, as they see it) and so she had yet another piano lesson after school next day, which suited me very well. I wanted to be free to go in pursuit of my quarry. I was more determined than ever to take an active role in whatever game this girl was playing with me. Next time she would not give me the slip so easily.

So I went into Stockbridge after I'd dropped my bag off at the house and began to saunter idly along the street, glancing in the shop windows. I would give her the chance to show herself, which I felt certain she would, and when she did I would be ready to pounce.

It was not long before she appeared. She came down the hill from the direction of the city centre and paused at the lights and at that moment Charlotte's mother said in my ear, 'Hello, Emily. You looked as if you were miles away there.'

I jumped. Mrs McDowell was standing in front of me, one hand resting on the handle of her tartan shopping trolley, eyeing me quizzically.

'Oh, Mrs McDowell, hello. Didn't see you there. I was just . . .' I had my eye still on the girl; she was waiting for the lights to change, and I must not lose her. 'Just, well, thinking.'

'So pleased you got your bike back, dear. It makes a change to find that someone's been honest in this day and age.'

'Oh, yes, yes it does.' The lights had changed. The girl was crossing the road and coming towards the bridge. The *Big Issue* seller held out a copy of the magazine to her, but she shook her head and kept on going. I was on the opposite side of the road.

'I must go, Mrs McDowell,' I said hurriedly. 'See you later.' I moved away without waiting for her response.

The girl had slowed her steps and begun to stroll in a leisurely way past the shops. It was possible that she had seen me when she was further up the hill. Once she had gone a little ahead of me I nipped smartly across the road, dodging a truck which honked at me noisily.

She had paused in front of the chemist's shop window. I made up the short distance between us and stopped behind her. We looked at each other's reflection in the window, mine clad in my school uniform, hers in jeans and a black top. I felt startled seeing us like this, our images overlapping. She smiled but I did not.

'Why have you been following me?' I asked.

'Have I?'

'You know you have.'

'If you say so.'

'I've seen you in the street where I live and outside my school.'

'It's a free world, ain't it? You don't own your street, do you? Not all of it. I've as much right to walk along it as you have.'

'I never said you hadn't.'

'Good.' Again came that smile. 'We see eye to eye then, don't we?'

We were looking at each other's eyes in the glass. I couldn't make out what colour hers were, but I suspected they might be hazel, like mine.

'What's your name?' I asked and for a moment was afraid she might say Emily, but she didn't.

'Eve.'

'I'm Emily.'

'I know that.'

'How do you?'

She shrugged.

'You've got to tell me who you are!'

'I already have. Hey, you're hurting my shoulder!'

I had put my hand on it, to make sure that she really existed and was not just something I had conjured up in my head to torment myself, but I hadn't realised that I was gripping her so hard. I let my arm drop.

'We must talk,' I said.

'Ain't that what we're doing?'

'You know what I mean.'

'Do I?'

'Let's go and have a coffee.' Sitting at a cafe table, drinking coffee, with other people around, would be something ordinary to do. It might be something that would defuse the situation, take it on to a more ordinary plane. But I had no confidence that she would accept. She gave me the feeling that she would always want to make the rules.

She considered, shrugged again. Then, 'Why not?' she murmured.

As we crossed the road I saw Charlotte's mother standing further along the pavement, gas-bagging to another woman. It takes her hours to get along the street, but by the time she gets home she knows all the news of the district. She saw me, so no doubt she noted my companion at the same time and would ask Charlotte later, 'Who's that girl with the dark hair that was with Emily this afternoon? She's not at your school, is she? She didn't look as if she would be.'

I took the girl with the dark hair so similar to my own to a basement cafe, one that Charlotte and I never went to. We were the only people there. We took a table in a dark corner, well away from the window, and I asked her what she would like.

'Whatever you're having.'

I ordered two coffees. Now that we were alone in a vacuum together like this I didn't know where to start, how to start. It had been easier in the street with the traffic providing background noise.

She said, 'Mind if I smoke?'

I shook my head. I'm sure she would have gone ahead whether I'd minded or not.

She brought out a packet of tobacco and some papers and began to roll a cigarette.

'Filthy habit, ain't it?'

I shrugged no.

'Don't suppose you do, do you?'

'No.'

'Thought not.' She licked the paper and then tapped the weedy-looking cigarette on the table top. 'Got any bad habits?'

'I guess I have. Who doesn't?'

'Tell me about them.'

'Why should I?' I was beginning to feel irritated. 'I don't know who you are or anything about you.'

She smiled, a bit like a cat confronting a mouse that it's playing with. Well, I wasn't going to let her play with me any further.

'Where are you from? You don't live in Edinburgh, do you?'

'Sure I do. I'm here, ain't I?'

'But before, where were you? London?'

'Good enough guess.'

'Why do you want to annoy me?'

'Do I?'

'You know you do. Admit it. But why should you want to? What have I ever done to you?' What could I have done? I had never set eyes on her until five or six days ago.

'Maybe *you*'ve not done much exactly.' She paused. 'But your dad now –'

I was more or less prepared for what was to come. I had lain awake half the night puzzling over it, coming to the only conclusion it seemed logical to come to.

'We're related, Emily,' she said softly. 'Don't you see, you're my sister?'

Chapter 5

Yes, I saw, of course I did. I saw it when I looked at her, sitting across the table from me there. I saw my father reflected in her face. I saw myself reflected.

But how had it come about? When? And where? A thousand questions rattled in my head.

'What age are you?' I had to find out first of all where she fitted in with me.

'Sixteen.' She blew out a stream of smoke. 'Naw, that's not true, it's what I tell people who are nosy and think I should be at school. I won't be sixteen until September.'

So she was three months older than me.

'I was in the picture before you, wasn't I?' She seemed pleased about that.

'I find it difficult –'

'What? To understand? It's not that difficult. Your dad fell in love with my mum. It was as easy as pie.'

'No!' I cried. 'How could that be?' He would have been married to my mother at that time and he was in love with her, wasn't he, of course he was, and always had been. Everyone said he was devoted to her.

'It just was. These things happen. He met my mum on a trip to London and he fell for her. She was lovely, was my mum.'

Was? I took a gulp of coffee.

'She died last year.'

I took another drink and said, 'I'm sorry,' though I didn't know whether I was or not. Possibly not. My brain felt numb, as if it was receiving messages it couldn't quite understand. But at least if this woman was dead she couldn't rear up and try to break our family apart.

'She was warm and soft was my mum, and good fun,' said Eve. I was trying to think of her with a name now, not just as *the girl*. My shadow. *Me and my shadow, Strolling down the avenue* . . . It was a song, an old one, and funnily enough I had a memory of my father singing it sometime way back in my childhood.

I sat looking at Eve, my *sister*. I had often fancied having a sister but had not imagined her coming in this way.

'So what have you been doing since then?' I asked. 'Since she –'

'Died?' She didn't shy away from the word as much as I did. 'I was supposed to stay with my mum's friend, Gloria. Not much glory in her. A right bitch she is. Couldn't stick her, so I ran away.'

It was a world a million miles away from mine, I didn't need anyone to spell that out for me. I found it difficult even to imagine.

I put my next question. 'How did my dad meet your mum?'

'In a pub.'

In a *pub*? 'Are you sure?'

'Sure I'm sure. My mum worked in a pub, in Stoke Newington. I don't suppose you know where that is?' I shook my head and she went on. 'North London. It's where we live. Lived. They clicked straight away, your dad and my mum.'

She seemed to enjoy saying that: your dad and my mum. She was enjoying my misery too, I could see that.

'Every time he came to London after that he came to see her. He couldn't stay away.'

Every time? So it hadn't been just one wild weekend, a mad fling which he had regretted as soon as he got home. I hesitated before asking the next question. 'How long did it last?'

'Couple of years.'

'A couple –' I fell silent. I felt as if the breath had been knocked out of me.

So for two years or perhaps more my father had been leading a double life, one in London and one here in Edinburgh with my mother. Was it true? Could I believe this girl? But when I looked at her and saw eyes so like my father's eyes and expressions so like my father's expressions how could I not? It was uncanny, the likeness between them, and I supposed, therefore, between her and me. For me, it was like finding a twin, a mirror image of myself, but one that I did not want.

'My mum really fell for your dad. Said he treated her royally, brought her flowers every time he came, chocolates too, sometimes a bottle of bubbly. She said he'd meant more to her than any other guy she'd ever known. She'd have given up anything for him.'

'But he wouldn't for her?'

'Typical, ain't it? That's men for you. My mum thought he really did love her but he had too much to lose up here. So when she got pregnant – with me – he backed off. He sent her a couple of hundred quid and that was that.'

'You never saw him then?'

'Once, though I don't remember it. My mum told me. I was only a year old. He came, he wanted to see me. He told my mother he had another daughter, called Emily. He said we were as alike as two peas in a pod. He said if it hadn't been for you he would have left your mum and come to mine.'

'I don't believe you!' I cried out.

'That's what he said.'

'Or what your mum said he said.'

'Take your pick.'

How could one know the truth of it all? I parked my elbows on the table and rested my face in my hands.

I didn't want to have to look her in the eye any longer, it was too unnerving. She rolled another cigarette and lit it.

'Shock for you, ain't it?'

'I suppose you must hate me?'

'Naw. Not really.'

I lifted my head. 'But you were following me.'

'I wanted to see how you lived, what kind of house you had, what kind of school you went to.'

She had wanted to see what kind of life she might have had if my father had opted for her and her mother instead of me and my mother.

I got up, bumping against the table leg and setting the coffee cups rattling in their saucers. My head was whirling. I had to go home, to check that my father would come back when he usually did and that everything would go on as it always had. I felt as if my life had been thrown into total confusion. Nothing was as I had thought it was. The devotion of my parents to each other. The orderliness of our lives. The trust I had always put in my father.

'I'll be around tomorrow,' said Eve, 'if you want to see me.'

I nodded and left, too choked up to say anything more. I hadn't even asked what had passed between my father and her when they'd met. But I knew I would have to see her again.

My mother wasn't yet home when I got in. I wanted to speak to my father and was tempted to ring him at his office. I sat in front of the phone, one finger on the receiver, wondering if I dared lift it. And then what? Ask him straight out. I couldn't do it. I just couldn't. While I was sitting there the phone began to ring, making me jump. I lifted the receiver nervously and almost dropped it when I heard my father's voice at the other end.

'Is that you, Emily? You sound a bit odd. Are you all right?'

My voice cracked as I said, 'Fine.'

'You don't sound it. Are you starting a sore throat?'

'No, no, I'm fine.'

He had rung to say he would be home later than usual. Pressure of work. We should go ahead and eat without him. Was it true, was it really pressure of work that was delaying him, or had he arranged to see Eve again? Or maybe he was meeting another woman, bringing her chocolates and flowers? For all I knew, he could have someone else in his life now.

'Are you sure you're all right?' he persisted.

'Yes,' I said, and, 'I must go. See you later.' I put the phone down. My hand was clammy. I dried it on the back of my school skirt. Then I heard the front door opening, signalling the return of my mother.

I told her my father had called and she said, 'I hope he's not forgotten that we're going to the opera.' The opera! I was sure he had. He doesn't like opera and goes along only to please my mother. 'I'd better give him a ring.' She dialled and got his secretary.

'Mandy,' she said, 'may I have a word with John, please?' She frowned as she listened to what Mandy had to say. 'Did he say when he would be back? No? Well, if he does come back tell him I phoned.' She replaced the receiver, still frowning. 'He left the office a few minutes ago.'

'Maybe he's on his way home,' I said, though I didn't believe it.

'I think he has some business worries, but you know your father, he keeps them to himself! He doesn't want to worry us.' She went off to have a shower and get dressed.

No, I didn't know my father and, what was more, she didn't either. The secret weighed on me like a ton of bricks, bowing me down. I wished I could share it with someone. Ben, preferably, but how could you start to tell anyone such a thing over the phone? *Hey, you'll never guess, Dad had another woman in London and he's got this daughter, spitting image of me*. Ben rang while my mother was in the shower and I asked when he'd next be back in Edinburgh.

'Two or three weeks probably.'

'Three weeks!'

'Are you all right, Em?'

'I'm fine,' I said dully. My head was so dull I'd been having a problem concentrating on my physics homework. 'Fine,' I repeated like a robot.

My mother came down and had a quick word with him. She was looking pretty snazzy in black silk – elegant, I guess, would be the correct word – and a whiff of perfume caught my nose as she went past. She smiled while she talked to Ben, but after she'd said goodbye to him she was back to frowning and looking at her watch.

'Where on earth can he be? I suppose you could come with me instead, Emily?'

'Me? Oh no, I don't think so. Look at me!' I felt grubby after a day at school. 'And I've got loads of homework to do.' That was one of the things in life my mother regarded as ultra-important, so I knew she'd let me off with that excuse. I don't like opera any more than my dad does, it's too heavy for me. Music's fine, drama's fine, but not the two together. And I find the plots daft. She says they're not meant to be realistic.

'I'll just have to go on ahead. I'll leave his ticket here, Emily –' she laid it on the kitchen table – 'and you can give it to him when he gets in. He'll be able to come in at the first interval. Surely he won't be any later than that.'

But he was. He didn't come home till ten.

'You were supposed to be at the opera,' I told him.

'The opera! Oh, my God!' He smote himself sharply on the forehead with the palm of his hand. 'Your mother will never forgive me.'

'No,' I said calmly, 'probably not.'

'It went clean out of my head.' He collapsed into a chair and closed his eyes.

'Do you want anything to eat?'

He shook his head. Mum had left something for him all ready to pop into the microwave. God's gift for wives with late husbands, that's what Mrs McDowell calls the microwave. My father said he'd had a sandwich in the office. Mandy had gone out and got it for him. I began to wonder about Mandy now. Could he be involved with her? No, of course not. The ideas passing through my head were getting crazier and crazier. Mandy was only twenty-five, *thirty* years younger than my father, and she already had a boyfriend, didn't she? I seemed to remember Dad mentioning one. But this was awful. Every time he'd come home late from now on my head would be buzzing with suspicions. I went to bed. I couldn't bear to look at him. And I didn't want to be around when my mother returned alone from the opera. For a start, the seats cost an arm and a leg, and someone else could have benefited from the free ticket if she had known in time. That in itself would annoy her. She hates waste.

I didn't feel up to seeing Eve the next day, so I stayed away from all the places I might run across her. I persuaded Charlotte to come to the baths with me. She enjoys swimming, so she didn't grumble too much. Afterwards, we went back to her house and drank hot chocolate and ate warm scones freshly made by her mother. Mrs McDowell doesn't go out to work so she has time for things like cooking and baking. Their house felt terribly normal. All the surfaces were dust-free and the smell in the kitchen was wholesome and comforting. And you could never imagine Mr McDowell having an affair with anybody.

In the evening, however, I didn't find much comfort. When I was sitting at my desk in the window struggling to do my French homework I looked out and saw my shadow standing on the opposite pavement under the overhanging branches of a lilac tree. It seemed there was to be no escaping her. She had said she didn't hate me, but she wanted to cause trouble, oh yes she did, a whole lot of trouble. We were going to have to pay for my father's desertion of her and her mother.

I thought I'd just let her stand there and get on with it. I wasn't going to run at her beck and call. My concentration was gone now though. Then I began to worry that my mother might catch sight of her and see the likeness herself and wonder. I got up and pushed my chair back. And as I did I heard the front door opening. My father emerged on to the path below in shirt and trousers. He went quickly to the gate and crossed the road to where Eve was standing.

He began to talk to her. His manner was urgent. Was he pleading with her? Was he asking her to go away and leave us alone? She was listening, head half bent, with an amused little smile. They would be visible to anyone like me who happened to be looking out of their window. And my mother? Where was she? I ran downstairs and found that she had finished tidying up the kitchen and was getting ready to go up to the drawing room on the first floor. I had to delay her until Dad came in. I asked her about a problem in my French homework. She speaks French fluently. She'd spent a year in Paris after she'd finished her studies, in the days before she met my father.

'Do you want to get your book?' she suggested. 'It might be easier if I could see the passage for myself.'

No, I didn't, I didn't want to leave her in case she followed me up to my room. I could remember the passage exactly, I said. I stalled her for as long as I could and then I ran out of steam.

'There's something on television I want to see for once!' she said, and opening the kitchen door she went ahead of me into the hall. At that moment the front door, which had been left ajar, swung in to admit my father.

'Have you been out, John?' asked my mother.

'Just checking the car.' Lies, lies, and more lies! He was looking flustered, as well he might.

I went back up to my room. I was going to see Eve tomorrow, to plead with her myself, to ask her to please, *please*, leave us alone. If it were money that she wanted I would offer her my savings. I had a thousand pounds in a building society account, put there by my grandparents on my mother's side to be a help towards my further education. As far as I was concerned, Eve could have it all.

Chapter 6

'Are you trying to bribe me?'

'Maybe.'

'Buy me off?' She was amused. 'That would be too easy, wouldn't it?'

'What do you want from us?' I demanded, then I lowered my voice for we were not the only people in the cafe. A woman at the next table was already taking too much interest in us. 'You want to destroy us, don't you? You'd like to break up our family!'

'Why do you think I'd want to do that?' She needn't think she could come over all innocent to me! Her tongue was lodged firmly in her cheek. 'You're getting angry, Emily. Because I've broken into your nice little world. But I'm your sister, remember! Don't you think I should have a place in your world?'

'Look, it's not my fault that your life has been harder than mine!'

'Did I say it was?'

If I was angry, so was she. She was filled with it, fuelled by it. Why else would she have come here?

I got up and went to the counter and asked to pay for two coffees. She followed me. The girl on the till said, 'Are you twins?'

'Almost,' said Eve. 'Everybody comments on the likeness.'

'That'll be two pounds,' said the girl.

I was fumbling in my purse for the coins but Eve had her wallet open. She reached across me and paid with a twenty pound Bank of Scotland note. I saw that she had a wad of others tucked into the back of the wallet. She wouldn't have picked that lot up begging at the Playfair Steps.

We left the cafe and she fell into step beside me.

'I've seen your place,' she said. 'Would you not like to see mine?'

'Do you have a place? Here, in Edinburgh?' The idea surprised me.

'You don't think I'm sleeping on the street do you?'

I hadn't given any thought to that aspect of her; she had been existing for me solely in her role as a stalker, someone who had been following me around on my territory. The only other context I had seen her in was as a beggar at the side of the art gallery, and that had seemed like an extension of her hounding me, not letting me go in peace anywhere I would normally go.

'Don't you want to?' she asked. 'See my place?'

Well, I did, to be honest. On one hand, I hated her for what she was doing to me and my family but, on the other, I was curious. I couldn't just walk away. I wanted to know this girl who was also my father's daughter. I wanted to try to understand her, find out how her mind worked. Apart from being related by blood it seemed that we had absolutely nothing in common. Her strangeness fascinated me.

'Come on,' she urged, 'be a devil!'

Still I hesitated, for I had no idea where she would lead me and I sensed it could be dangerous to get embroiled in her life. Her invitation, though, was one I could not resist.

'OK,' I said.

'Let's go then!'

'Now?' I looked down at my school uniform. I'd have preferred to have been wearing jeans; it would have put me more on a level with her. In school uniform she made me feel like a kid.

'You look classy kitted out like that,' she said with her half-smile. 'And don't worry! You're frowning but you're not going to your doom. I'm not going to take you into a lion's den. We're just going for a ride out into the country.' She would say no more.

We walked up to Princes Street and boarded a bus. We sat up on the top deck. As we bowled through the streets she became talkative.

'I like Edinburgh, yeah, I really do. Does that surprise you? Not like London of course, doesn't have the same buzz, and the people aren't too free with their dosh. Well, except for the odd one,' she said meaningfully. 'London's no better that way, mind you. So I think I might stick around for a while. Get to know the place better. Get to know the people better.'

I said nothing, I let her prattle on. I was wondering where we were going. We went through the inner suburbs and then the outer suburbs. We went to the end of the line. I hadn't believed her when she'd said we were going for a ride in the country. I wouldn't have imagined her in the middle of green fields. But that was where she was taking me.

She took me to a caravan park.

'Ever lived in a van?'

I shook my head. We'd spent a week in one once on the west coast when Ben and I were small and it had rained all week and the midges had been murder and I'd had a cough. At the end of it my mother had said never again! It was my father who had wanted to do it; he had memories of spending a week in the very same place with his parents when the sun had shone non-stop and he'd paddled and collected shells. It was the only holiday he'd ever had as a boy. Afterwards, he'd said of course it was stupid to try to repeat things and he should have known that.

'It's good, living here,' said Eve, leading me between the vans, most of which looked shut up. The walkways were paved and the place seemed well kept. 'You can hear the birds in the morning. Hell of a racket they make but that's all right. It's a nice kind of noise. Better than being in a dirty squat. They've got showers and loos here too.' She had always looked clean when I'd seen her, except when she'd been wrapped in the dirty grey blanket.

Her caravan was at the back of the park, beside a high privet hedge.

'Gives us privacy,' she said. 'Don't like people looking in on us. Guess you don't either?'

'Not particularly.'

The van was oldish-looking, smaller and less streamlined than most of the others, some of which were almost as big as bungalows. I presumed the rent of this one would be cheaper.

'When I've got enough dosh I'm going to buy myself a really crack van and park it beside the sea somewhere. Then I can tell the rest of the world to sod off.'

Would she look to my father for the dosh? The notes in her wallet must have come from him.

She tugged open the van door and called, 'Lenny?'

She didn't live alone! I hadn't quite registered the 'us' and I'd forgotten about her begging partner. He rose up from a bunk where he'd been lying prostrate smoking a joint. The van smelt of pot.

'I've brought Emily home,' said Eve.

'Good for you! Welcome, Emily, to our humble abode!' He made me a deep bow.

Now I felt really nervous and was tempted to turn and run but I knew I'd be followed by their mocking laughter if I did. Perhaps they might not even let me go. I'd been a fool to come.

'It's all right, Emily,' said Eve. 'Lenny might look fierce, but he doesn't bite.'

'Sez who?' He bared his teeth, which looked in need of dental attention, and gave a short laugh that sounded more like a bark. He had a sharp face and a wispy beard and his small, glittery eyes made me think of a ferret. There was the dog, too, the mangy one they'd been begging with. He lay sprawled on his side, snoring, chained to a hook on the wall. I swallowed. My throat felt grainy. My parents would have had a fit if they could have seen me. My parents! I'd forgotten about them.

'Come in, come in,' cried Lenny, clearing clothes from a seat. 'We're honoured. Take a pew!'

I took one, sitting gingerly on the edge of it.

'Want a coffee?' asked Eve.

I cleared my throat and managed to say, 'Please.'

She filled the kettle and spooned instant coffee into three mugs. 'Sorry we don't rise to the proper stuff. Don't suppose you ever have instant coffee at home?'

'Sometimes.' It was a lie. My mother wouldn't have it in the house. Why should she if she doesn't like it? I felt I was trying to defend her in my head.

'Eve tells me you live in a posh house?' said Lenny, throwing the end of his joint into the sink where it sizzled for a moment. 'Roses in the garden and all that jazz.'

What was I to say to that? I shrugged.

'Eve likes roses, don't you, Eve? Maybe Emily'll bring you some roses from her garden.'

The dog suddenly lifted his head and snorted and then seeing me, a stranger, sitting there, snarled, showing his few yellow teeth. He had probably tuned into my nervousness. They say dogs can sense it. I shifted my feet to the left, out of his reach.

'Go and take Jason out, Lenny,' said Eve. 'He needs a walk. He stinks.'

'And leave you girls to have a heart to heart?' Lenny unhooked the chain and jingled it and Jason struggled to his feet. 'Right then, boy, out!'

Lenny and Jason lumbered down the van steps. Eve left the door open. 'Need some fresh air in here. That dog doesn't half pong. I'd like to get rid of it. It belongs to Lenny. He says it protects us. Fat lot of use it'd be in a tight corner. Only got four teeth. I thought of trying to lose it somewhere, like under a fast-moving truck.'

'Lenny might not like it.'

'That's what's stopped me so far. I'd have to work it out so as he wouldn't know who'd done it. He's got a hot temper has Lenny.'

'Why do you stay with him then?'

She looked at me with surprise as if that wouldn't be a reason to leave someone. 'I can have a temper myself at times. What about yourself?'

'At times.' But it wasn't a violent temper, not any more. I'd learned to control that in my early childhood. If I wanted to take it out on somebody or something I punched my pillow until my fist hurt. But Eve and Lenny, what would they do? Take it out on each other?

'How long have you been with him?'

'Three or four months. Met him in a squat.'

'A squat? Did you really live in one?'

'Did I really live in one?' said Eve, aping my voice. 'Yeah, I really did. Fancy that. Disgusts you, doesn't it? Only dirty people live in squats, don't they? No-hopers. No-goods.'

I knew she was trying to rile me, but I felt my face heating up nevertheless. 'It's just . . .' I began, floundering. 'It's just, well, I haven't known anyone who's lived in a squat.'

'That's cos you've lived such a rosy, cosy little life.' Her voice was so sharp now it would have cut you like a razor. 'A privileged little life where Daddy'll see you don't come to any harm.'

My own temper flared. 'It's not my fault I've been privileged. It's an accident what you're born into. Fate. What am I supposed to do? Bring half a dozen homeless people home, tell them, "Make yourselves at home, use our house as a squat"? It wouldn't have a hope in hell of working.'

'Not for you maybe. But the homeless'd like it. All those nice roses in the garden. It'd spoil your little life though, wouldn't it?'

I jumped up and seized my bag.

'Not leaving, are you?'

'I'm not going to sit here listening to you slagging me off. You said you didn't hate me but you bloody well do.'

'Swearing now, are we? Tut-tut. Mummy wouldn't like it, would she?'

I almost hit her. I could have done but I pulled back just in time. The knowledge made me tremble. I made a move towards the door but she seized my arm and held me back.

'Don't go, please don't, Emily! I'm sorry. I've got a stupid mouth. I want us to be friends.'

I hesitated. At least she'd had to apologise to me and drop her aggressive attitude, though I was aware that probably wouldn't last.

'There's things I want to tell you. To show you. Please, Emily. I don't want you to go now that I've found you.'

'All right.' I sighed and sat down again, knowing that if I were sensible I would just get up and go and have nothing more to do with her.

'Where were we, before that little bit of trouble?'

'You were telling me how you met Lenny.'

'Oh yes. When he heard I had business up in Edinburgh he said he'd go with me. He'd always wanted to go to Scotland. His grandad was Scottish so we had that in common. He was Scottish, wasn't he, our dad's father?'

It still gave me a shock to hear her saying that so matter-of-factly. *Our dad*.

'Is he dead, our grandad? And our grandma?'

'They died quite a long time ago.'

'Pity that. I'd have liked to have known them. I don't have any relations on my mother's side. My mum was an orphan.'

'I'm sorry,' I muttered. I didn't tell her about Aunt Etta in case she'd target her next. That could really set the cat among the pigeons, as the saying goes.

'That's her there. My mum.' Eve took a framed photograph down from a ledge and wiped the glass on her sleeve. She studied it for a moment, then passed it to me.

I looked into the face of the woman my father had once loved. She had blonde hair and her head was thrown back as if she had just been laughing. Her eyes appeared to follow me when I moved my head to the side. If it wasn't for you, she seemed to be saying, I'd have lived with your dad and had a good life and given my daughter a good life and she wouldn't have to sit on the pavement begging. I couldn't imagine this woman begging, though. She looked too positive, too alive, for that. I handed the photograph back to her daughter.

'She's –'

'She's what?' persisted Eve.

'Pretty.'

'More than that. She was beautiful.'

Eve was right. There was a kind of radiance about the face.

'Got one or two more photos here that you might be interested in.' She took them from a crumpled envelope and passed them over to me.

The first one gave me a shock that was so sharp I felt I'd touched an electric wire. There was my father's face staring up at me, side by side with Eve's mum! He had his arm round her shoulders and they were both smiling. It had been taken against the background of a bar. That was it, the ultimate and final proof from which there was no escaping.

'Nice picture, ain't it? That was in me mum's pub.'

I turned it over. Underneath was a photograph of my father on his own, glass in hand, seated on a high bar stool. It was obvious that he was looking at the person on the other side of the counter. He was smiling.

I passed the photographs back.

'I used to look at these when I was little and I'd think, when I grow up I'm going to go and find him, my dad.'

And what now that she had found him? I was afraid to ask and suspected she would reveal nothing of her plans if I did.

'How did you find us?'

'No problem. Mum had told me my dad was a property man. Lenny looked him up on the Net for me – Lenny's brilliant with computers, you wouldn't think so, would you? – you can find anything you want on the Net. And your address was in the phone book, well, that made it dead easy, didn't it?'

'I guess it did.'

I rose, saying I had to go. I'd had enough to take in at present.

'Come again, eh? You don't have to be afraid of Lenny, you know. He won't hurt you.'

I didn't commit myself one way or the other. I wanted to leave quickly now, and be away before the return of Lenny and his dog, who both made me feel uneasy.

Eve offered to walk me to the bus stop, but I said that wasn't necessary.

'Thanks for the coffee.'

'You're real polite, aren't you? Even when you don't want to be.'

A thought suddenly occurred to me. 'Have you mentioned me to my father? Have you told him that you've seen me?'

'Our father,' she corrected. I inclined my head in acceptance of the fact. 'No, I haven't,' she added. I didn't think she would have done, but I'd had to ask, otherwise I wouldn't have known where I stood with him.

I said, 'See you!' For no doubt I would, one way or another. She watched me from the door of the van as I walked briskly away; I could feel her eyes on my back. I went through the caravan park to the main road without seeing any sign of Lenny and Jason or of anyone else. The place felt eerily deserted. I had to wait a while for a bus which, when it did come, took ages getting through town as it was the rush hour, but I didn't mind as I needed time to try to come to terms with what I'd learned that afternoon.

My mother was home before me. 'Where have you been?' she asked.

'Up town.' The lie tripped off my tongue without any effort. It wasn't a total lie, anyway.

'You didn't go to your violin lesson.'

'I forgot!' I had been having violin lessons for four years, scraping away on it, literally, for I really wasn't much good, I knew that and my teacher knew that, but my mother wouldn't accept it. She said it was good to be able to play a musical instrument and one should not give up without first persevering. To begin with, I had been quite keen, then had gone off it.

'Miss McLean rang, wondering where you were.'

'I'm sorry.'

'So am I. I have to pay her whether you go or not.'

'I'll pay her out of my allowance.'

'Don't be silly.'

'I don't want to go back,' I said suddenly and definitely. 'And you can't force me to.'

'No, of course I can't,' said my mother reasonably. She is seldom unreasonable when it comes to it. Sometimes I would even prefer her to prolong an argument, so that I could purge my feelings, as it were. 'Nor would I want to. There'd be no point. But I'm disappointed, Emily. If you'd put your mind to it in the beginning you could have been playing quite well by now.'

'I'm sorry,' I muttered, and turned to go upstairs.

'What have you got on the back of your skirt, Emily?'

I stopped and tried to peer round at it. My mother came closer to do an inspection.

'You're covered with hairs! Dog hairs, by the look of it. Where on earth did you pick those up?'

'I don't know. Must have been some seat.'

'Seems odd, if you were just up town. You'll need to give it a good brush.' She handed me a clothes brush. 'What *has* got into you lately, dear? I saw Marian' – that was Mrs McDowell, Charlotte's mother – 'and she said Charlotte thinks you've not been yourself either. You've always been so close. You're not going off Charlotte now, are you?'

'Of course not.'

I took the brush up to my room and closed the door behind me. I removed my skirt and brushed it vigorously. I could smell Jason on the hairs. Even after I'd removed as many of the hairs as I possibly could without reducing the skirt to a threadbare rag, it still smelt of the dog, and Eve's caravan. I resolved never to go back, but even in the middle of making the resolution I doubted if I would be able to keep it.

Chapter 7

Our meals had become tense affairs. It was as if we wanted to get through them as fast as possible so that we could leave the table and get away from one another. Usually we talked a lot, about school or my parents' work or the play Ben was currently involved in, anything that came up. My mother did her best, but she had two leaden weights to contend with, neither of which she could quite comprehend. My father was continuing to look preoccupied and my head was permeated with thoughts of my half-sister and her life in a caravan with a man called Lenny and a smelly dog called Jason. I didn't know how long my head could contain all of that without bursting.

'I got the confirmation for our bookings to France this morning,' said my mother. We had just finished eating.

'France?' My father raised his head. 'Oh yes, of course.'

'Are we going to France?' I asked.

'Do you never listen, Emily?' My mother spoke good-naturedly, however. 'We're going at the end of July, you surely haven't forgotten that? For two weeks. We're taking a *gîte* in the Cévennes. I thought you might like to ask Charlotte to come with us.'

'I'm not sure. She might be doing something else. She mentioned Crete, I think.'

What if I were to say, 'I've got this friend Eve, why don't we ask her to come with us?' Was she my friend? Or my foe? I was unable to decide, though thought it was more likely to be the latter.

'Why don't you ask her?'

'Who?'

'Charlotte, of course!' My mother's patience was slipping.

'Yes, all right, I will.'

'I'm looking forward to getting away,' said my father, laying a hand on top of my mother's where it rested on the table top. 'I could do with a break.'

'I think you could.' Her fingers curled to interlock with his.

They smiled at each other.

I couldn't stand it another minute. Little did my mother know! I got up and started to clear the dirty dishes, making a considerable clatter.

'Steady, Emily,' reproved my mother.

'Yes, no need to break up the happy home,' said my father.

Happy home indeed! If he knew what I knew he wouldn't joke so easily. Hypocrite! I longed to shout it in his face, but I kept quiet and sullenly carried the plates into the kitchen. I felt so angry! I felt like throwing the plates across the room and watching them break into splinters against the newly painted white wall. But I had been taught to control my temper. I wondered if Eve had and what she would do if she were provoked.

I set to work stacking the dishwasher and as I did I hummed 'Me and My Shadow'. The words ran constantly through my head. I was so gathered into my own thoughts that I didn't register my father coming into the kitchen until he was behind me and had taken up the refrain.

'*Me and my shadow, Strolling down the avenue,*' he sang. 'Do you remember the next bit?' He carried on, '*Me and my shadow, Not a soul to tell one's troubles to.*'

He could say that again! I kept my head down and continued stacking the plates. I didn't think I could look him in the eye.

'By the way, Emily, I saw your Aunt Etta today.'

I straightened up. I noticed that he'd closed the door behind him.

'She said she'd seen you down at Leith on Sunday?'

I ran the tap and began to wash my hands.

'She said you were looking for your bike.'

'I was.'

'But you told us you'd left it outside the Botanics?'

'I'd sort of left it there.'

'It's a long way from the Botanic Garden to Leith, Emily.'

So he was worried, was he, in case I might have seen him? Well, let him worry. This mess we were in was all his fault and I was beginning to hate him for it.

'Maybe it was a little bit of a white lie.' Now I did look him in the eye.

'So what *were* you doing down at Leith on Sunday?'

The door opened and my mother came in. I stared at my father daring him to repeat his question but he did not. I knew he couldn't afford to. My mother glanced at him and then at me sensing that something was going on.

'Shall we have some coffee?' she suggested in a bright tone of voice.

'Good idea,' said my father.

'Not for me,' I said, and left them to it.

'She is being rather trying at present, John,' I heard my mother say as I went up the stairs. Her voice carried even though she was trying to keep it down. I paused to listen to what he would say in response.

'I wouldn't worry too much, Mary. You know it's a difficult age, fifteen. I dare say it'll pass, whatever it is.'

Would it indeed? How did you make another real-life flesh-and-blood fifteen-year-old daughter pass? She wasn't going to disappear into the mist, however much he might wish it. Did he wish it? I was struck by the thought that, however big a complication she might present in his life, he might have been delighted to see her, this daughter of the woman he had loved so much that he had been prepared to put his own marriage in jeopardy. He might come to prefer her over me.

Next day, after school, when Charlotte suggested going for coffee, I said I couldn't.

'Why not?' She wouldn't let me go without a good excuse. I told her I'd promised to go and visit Aunt Etta.

'What do you want to visit her for?'

'She's my aunt, isn't she?'

'I promised Mark and Donald we'd meet them.'

'You go on your own then.'

'I don't want to go on my own. Why don't you come for a coffee first and then go and see your Aunt Etta? You said you'd be free this afternoon.'

'When did I say that?'

'Yesterday. Or don't you remember?'

We were on the edge of a spat – about nothing! Or was it about an issue other than me not going for coffee with her? I think she sensed I was up to something and was excluding her. She was pursing her lips. She was in a huff.

'You don't usually bother much about your Aunt Etta, do you?'

'How do you mean?' I was getting annoyed now.

'Well, she wasn't even asked to your parents' anniversary party.'

'She'd have felt out of place,' I said uncomfortably. That was what my mother had said when Dad had tentatively suggested it. He'd agreed straight away, saying she was probably right. And, to be honest, who would Aunt Etta have wanted to talk to in that crowd? I found some of them hard going myself even though I'd known them for years.

'She didn't get a chance to find out though, did she?' said Charlotte.

'It's none of your business, Charlotte!'

We parted frostily. It had happened before. How could you be friends with someone for fifteen years and not have the odd spat? I went home and changed and took out my bike. I cycled down to Leith, for I hadn't lied to Charlotte when I'd told her I was going to visit my aunt.

I rang her bell and waited, my ear close to the grille beside the door.

'Yes?' Her voice came floating out of it sounding a little suspicious. She was constantly on her guard for con men trying to get access to her flat, pretending to be from the water board or gas board. Her friend Doreen had got caught out that way.

'It's Emily,' I returned.

'Oh, Emily! Push the door, love!'

When I heard the catch being released I pushed the door and entered the dark passage. There was a vague smell of tomcat, there always was. I chained my bike to the bottom railing – I wasn't going to be caught out a second time – and began to climb. The stair goes up four flights and there are three flats to a landing, so a lot of people live here and more than one has cats. My father had offered to buy her a nice modern flat in one of the new developments, but she preferred it here.

Aunt Etta lives on the second floor. She was waiting for me at her door.

'Emily, this is a lovely surprise!' She greeted me with open arms and took me inside. In spite of the mildness of the day she had her gas fire in the living-kitchen turned up full. It's one of those with mock coals that looks like an open fire. I removed my jacket and took the armchair furthest away from the heat. The small room is stuffed with furniture and every ledge is covered with small china ornaments. Shepherdesses, cats, dogs, presents from Blackpool and Morecambe and the Algarve that people have brought back for her.

'Now what can I get you? You'll be hungry after a day at school. I'm out of bacon but I have some lovely sausages fresh from the butcher this morning.'

There was no point in protesting for she was already lighting the gas and putting the frying pan on the ring. The oil sputtered as she tossed in the sausages. She made us two apiece which we ate tucked inside floury white rolls and drank with tea that was piping hot and dark. What with the warm room and the food (which tasted brilliant) I could have gone to sleep. I wanted to talk to her but I didn't know where to start.

'How's your dad?' she asked, giving me my opening.

'Well, as a matter of fact, I'm worried about him.'

'Working too hard as usual, I suppose?'

'Yes, of course. What's new? But I kind of think something else is bothering him. Aunt Etta, he talks to you, doesn't he?'

'Sometimes.' She was looking guarded now.

'He's been acting a bit oddly. And then there was this phone call –'

'He doesn't go into his phone calls with me.' She got up abruptly and, gathering our dirty plates, she took them to the sink. She stood there with her back to me washing them under the running tap and I thought, *She knows. He's told her!* But can I tell her that I know?

'Has he been up to see you?' I asked.

'I'll need to be getting on, Emily. I'm going to the pictures with Doreen and I've still to get changed. Sorry about this, dear. It was lovely seeing you, though. Mind and come again.'

She almost shovelled me out the door in her eagerness to get rid of me. I descended the stairs slowly and thoughtfully and tripped over a cat that scuttled past yowling as if a pack of hounds was after it. Had my father told Aunt Etta about his affair when it was going on all those years ago? He might well have done. He'd have needed to confide in somebody. So the chances were that Aunt Etta knew, and I knew. But my mother, the person it would affect most, did not.

I unlocked my bike and wheeled it out into the street and all but bumped into my shadow.

'Did you follow me?' I could feel my temper getting up.

But how could she have followed me, when I'd been on my bike? It was impossible to keep track of her or guess her movements. She appeared and reappeared like someone with supernatural powers. Maybe she was a witch! But I don't believe in witches, at least not on the whole.

'So happens I know our Aunt Etta lives here.' She pointed to the name beside the bell. 'I saw our dad going in and put two and two together.'

'How did you know about Aunt Etta in the first place?'

'My mum knew, didn't she? She said he was very fond of his sister, Etta, always talked a lot about her. Said he owed her. She'd more or less brought him up when his mum was going out to work.'

I began to walk off, pushing my bike along the pavement in an effort to get her to move away from the door. Aunt Etta's friend Doreen might arrive at any moment and think she was seeing double! Eve followed.

'Funny, isn't it, all of us Es,' she mused. 'Emily, Eve and Etta.'

Three females in my dad's life. She didn't have to point out that my mother's name Mary was the odd one out.

When we were round the corner I turned and faced Eve. 'Have you been bothering Aunt Etta?'

'How do you mean bothering? She's my aunt too, isn't she? Haven't I as much right as you to visit her?'

'No, I wouldn't say you had.'

'Opinions might differ on that. I met her first a long time ago. She came to visit me and my mum once in London. I was about five. She came from your dad to find out how we were and bring presents.'

This girl was capable of delivering one shock after another.

'She liked my mum.' That was a loaded remark too. *But she doesn't like yours.*

'She didn't come again. My mum said she thought Aunt Etta was afraid of getting too attached to us.'

'Why don't you go back to where you came from?' I demanded in a low but fierce voice. I felt furious with her for bringing such disruption into our lives.

She merely smiled.

Chapter 8

I just had to go back to Aunt Etta's the next day. When I announced this it caused another blip in my relationship with Charlotte.

'You're going back to see your aunt *again?*' I should have made up some other excuse. Charlotte was eyeing me curiously.

'I promised to take something down to her.' It was only another half-lie.

She shrugged. 'Doesn't matter. Hilary Adams asked me to play tennis with her. I thought I might.'

I decided I'd better try to soften her up a bit. 'By the way, Charlie,' I said, calling her back, for she had started to walk off, 'Mum was wondering if you'd like to come to France with us at the end of July for a couple of weeks? We're renting a *gîte*.'

'End of July? I'm not sure. I'll need to see.'

OK, suit yourself! I thought. She can be as stubborn as a mule at times, my best friend. I was too wrapped up in my own concerns to be too troubled. When all this blew over – when my shadow left town and I could walk alone again! – Charlotte and I would get back on our old footing. I didn't know if I'd ever be able to tell her about Eve. Possibly not. It would be a big secret for her to carry, one that she would more likely than not let spill out to her mother. And once Mrs McDowell had hold of it you might as well put out a broadcast on BBC Radio Scotland.

So Charlotte went off in a huff yet again and I cycled down to Leith. This time when I rang the bell Aunt Etta's voice sounded more cautious than it had the day before.

'It's Emily.'

There was a pause and then she said, 'I'm rather busy at the moment, Emily.' By listening hard I was just able to make out what she'd said.

'Can I come up for a minute or two, *please*, Aunt Etta? It's urgent.'

The door buzzed and I shoved it in before she'd change her mind. I padlocked the bike and raced up the stairs taking two and three at a time. They'd been recently washed and I slipped halfway up and went down on one knee. I cursed, though not too loudly. Aunt Etta wasn't waiting at her door this time but it was ajar so I went on in and found her sitting by the fire.

'I'm a bit troubled with my stomach today.'

'Oh, I'm sorry, Aunt Etta.' Then, straight away, without even sitting down, I said, 'I know all about Eve.'

'You do?' She was startled.

'She didn't tell you?'

Aunt Etta shook her head. She was wily, was Eve, and she played her cards close to her chest, revealing only what she wanted to reveal to each person caught up in her game.

'But you've seen her, haven't you?'

'Aye, she came up a day or two back. But how is it you know about her? Your dad's not said anything, has he?'

'Oh no!' I sat down and told Aunt Etta about Eve following me.

'She's a mixed-up lassie right enough.'

'Mixed up? She's downright dangerous!'

'She's not had an easy life, mind.'

'Not as easy as mine?' I could do without having that tune played in my ear again.

'Now I didn't say that, Emily. Don't go putting words in my mouth. You're in a bit of a tizzy, aren't you? Why don't you sit down and I'll make you a wee cup of something?'

I said I didn't want anything but I did sit down. 'She's trying to destroy us, Aunt Etta, don't you see?'

Aunt Etta sighed and stared at the hot coals in the gas fire. Was she on Eve's side? Were there sides to be taken?

'We've got to keep it from Mum,' I said.

'I don't know if that'll be possible, Emily.'

'The shock would kill her.'

'That's an exaggeration. Your mother's stronger than that.'

'But it might kill, well, what she *feels* for Dad.' It might be the end of a happy marriage. The end of a happy family. My mother valued truth so highly, along with honesty and loyalty. Nobody could knock virtues like those. She might never be able to forgive my father.

'At some point he may have to tell her,' said Aunt Etta, 'but he'd want to do it when it suited him.'

'Not with Eve holding a gun to his head?'

Aunt Etta nodded. 'I've not told him Eve's been up to see me. I've not seen him since. But I don't think I'm going to tell him. He's got enough on his mind.' She agreed not to tell him that I had seen Eve, either. So here we were, circling around each other with our secrets!

'What are we to do?' I cried out in frustration. It was so infuriating not to be able to do anything, to be on the receiving end of this girl's whims, not knowing which way she would jump next.

Aunt Etta said she was trying to persuade Eve to go back to London, now that she'd seen her father and had a chance to talk to him. 'I told her straight out, I didn't mince my words, "There's nothing here for you." What kind of life could there be? I gave her the train fare to London.'

'She took it? She's had money from Dad as well. Maybe that's what she's come for.' But I knew money was not the whole of it. My offer of the thousand pounds in my building society account was still hanging in the air. She'd neither accepted nor refused it so far. If she did decide to accept it I wasn't sure if I could go through with handing it over. What would I say to my mother when she found out that the balance in my building society account stood at zero?

Aunt Etta and I chewed the problem over, going round in circles. The only thing we knew for sure was that it was essential, one way or another, to try to reason with Eve and persuade her to leave town. I wasn't convinced, however, that she was a person who could see reason. And even if we did persuade her to go, what was to stop her from coming back?

'Aunt Etta,' I said, 'about Dad's affair with Eve's mother –'

My aunt shifted uncomfortably on her seat. 'Your dad talked to me in confidence, Emily.'

'I know, but that was years ago. The picture's changed now, hasn't it? Talk to me about it, *please*! I want to try to understand. Did he really fall in love with this woman?'

'He was taken by her, certainly. Her name was Joyce. She was beautiful.'

'But, Aunt Etta, Mum's beautiful too.'

'It's not the whole of it, it never is, is it, the way someone looks?'

'So what did Joyce have that my mother didn't?'

'Maybe that he could relax with her. She was fun.'

'*Fun?* Is that all?' It made my father seem shallow, yet I knew he wasn't. Or had I had the wrong impression of him all along?

'Of course it wasn't. Joyce was a warm sort of woman who laughed a lot, the kind of person that draws people to her.'

'She's not like her daughter, then!'

Nor like my mother, whom people tend to find reserved until they get to know her.

'You can never quite explain these things, can you, Emily?' said Aunt Etta. 'Another part of it was that

Joyce had come from a similar background to us. She understood your dad, accepted him as he was, whereas your mum –'

My mother had moulded my father over the years, quietly and unobtrusively, into being the kind of husband she wanted to have. I saw that clearly now.

'I'm not saying anything against your mum, Emily. She's a fine woman, and a good woman. We might not see eye to eye all the time but that's neither here nor there.'

'Dad did love her though, when he married her, didn't he?'

'I'm sure he did. And he felt guilty, naturally enough, about Joyce.'

And he'd probably felt guilty ever since about abandoning Joyce and her daughter.

I didn't stay much longer. I wanted to be home before my mother so that she wouldn't have to ask me where I'd been. I was having to resort to too many lies and felt it was only a matter of time before I got caught out. But I was unlucky for it was rush hour and the traffic was murderous – every week it seems to double in the city – and even with a bike, which is easier to manoeuvre than a car, I had to be patient and wait along with everybody else. At times I resorted to pushing it along the pavement, but that didn't help much.

I saw that my mother's car was parked outside the house when I turned into our street. She was in the kitchen waiting for the kettle to boil. The first thing she does when she gets home is make a cup of tea.

'You look hot,' she observed.

'I've been for a run on my bike.'

'A run? In rush-hour traffic?'

These were not idle questions so I decided I'd better stick as close to the truth as possible.

'I was down Leith way so I called in to see Aunt Etta.'

'I heard you'd gone to visit her.' She'd met Mrs McDowell, well, of course she had. 'Charlotte said you went yesterday as well?'

'Is there a law against it?' I asked, and walked out of the kitchen and up the stairs to my room. That had not been a smart thing to say. Apart from annoying her, it would only make her ponder. She didn't mention it when I went back downstairs, but she was wearing her thoughtful look, which always makes me feel she can see right through me.

My father phoned to say he would be late home and not to wait dinner for him. My mother and I ate together in the kitchen. We had a chicken and fennel casserole which she had taken from the deep freeze. She's very well prepared always, she has to be, with a full-time, demanding job like hers. She has big cooking sessions at weekends and puts meals in the freezer. Sometimes I help her with the chopping of the vegetables. Even my father has been known to help. He's not helpless when it comes to chores and he makes a good pasta. He had to help in the house when he was a boy.

'So how was your Aunt Etta?' asked my mother as we settled down to eat.

'Her stomach was troubling her,' I said, glad to have some detail to report.

'Has she been to the doctor?'

We had a desultory conversation about Aunt Etta's stomach. We were not relaxed with each other and I wasn't very hungry though I was doing my best to clear my plate. I wondered what Eve and Lenny would be eating in their smelly caravan. Not chicken and fennel casserole anyway, I could be sure about that.

My mother finished ahead of me and so, when the phone rang and she said, 'No, don't get up, I'll go, finish your dinner,' it was difficult for me to argue. 'It's probably only a call centre,' she added. 'It's maddening the way they always phone at mealtimes. I must do something about getting the calls stopped.'

She left the room and I finished my dinner like a good little girl, resisting the temptation to put the last bit in the bin. Not because it tasted bad, only because I felt 'off my food'. Perhaps I had inherited Aunt Etta's dodgy tum. I seemed to have inherited her liking for sausage and bacon rolls. Not my mother's cup of tea at all. We only have wholemeal bread in our house. We eat healthily, which is not something to despise.

I was clearing the plates into the dishwasher when my mother returned to say, 'It's for you, Emily. A girl called Eve.'

Chapter 9

I let a dinner plate slip through my hands. It met the ground before I could catch it, and broke into two clean halves. The shock of hearing my mother pronounce Eve's name had been too much for me. It seemed to bring her right into the centre of our kitchen.

'Sorry,' I muttered, bending to pick up the pieces. Fortunately it was only a kitchen plate and not a piece of her prized Wedgwood.

'Give them to me. I'll wrap them up and put them in the bin. You'd better get the phone. She'll be waiting.'

The receiver was lying on the hall table. I lifted it gingerly as if it might electrocute me. 'Yes?' I barked.

'Hi, Sis, what's up with you? You didn't sound very friendly there. Aren't you pleased to hear me?'

'What do you think you're doing?' I had to speak in as quiet a voice as possible. The kitchen door was ajar and my mother is not hard of hearing.

'Phoning you, d'you mean?'

'Yes.'

'Sorry if I've called at an inconvenient time.'

'You have.'

'I just wanted to hear your voice. I missed you this afternoon. I was looking for you down at Stockbridge. I saw your pal, the one with the red hair, so I asked her where you were.'

I groaned.

'I want to see you, Emmie. Want to talk to you. We've got to talk more. We've only just got going. Why don't you come out to the caravan site tomorrow? We can talk better there.'

'I can't make tomorrow. I'm busy all weekend.'

'OK. How about Monday after school?'

'I'll see,' I said and clapped the receiver back on to its rest. I dialled 1471 to see if I could work out where she was phoning from, but the message said the caller had withheld their number. She'd probably been in a call box, anyway. And presumably she was not with my father. *Our* father.

I went back into the kitchen.

'Strawberries?' said my mother, spooning them into small glass dishes. 'I think we might allow ourselves a little cream, don't you? Could you get it out of the fridge?'

I put it on the table. We sat down to eat our dessert.

'Who's Eve?' asked my mother. 'I don't think I've heard you mention her before? Is she at school?'

'She's just an acquaintance. I don't know her very well.'

My mother let that go, but she would remember the name.

The phone rang again as we were finishing and I galloped into the hall to take it. But it was Charlotte this time and she seemed to have forgotten, at least temporarily, that she was annoyed with me.

'You know that girl who you said was following you? Well, she stopped me today and asked me where you were. She looks rather like you, doesn't she? Something odd about her though, don't you think so? Who is she, anyway? What's she after?'

'Listen, Charlotte –' I lowered my voice '– don't mention her to your mother, OK?'

'OK,' echoed Charlotte, and then she added defensively, 'I don't tell my mother everything, you know.' She might not intend to, but Mrs McDowell was brilliant at weaseling out information. She'd have done well as an interrogator for the Spanish Inquisition. She wouldn't have had to resort to pulling out toenails.

I looked round and saw that my mother was standing in the kitchen doorway. I'm sure she hadn't been eavesdropping – she's too principled for that (unlike me). She would merely have paused, not wanting to interrupt my call.

'Must go, Charlie, see you Monday,' I said and put down the phone. I waited for my mother to ask me the question *What is it you don't want Charlotte to tell her mother?*, but she didn't. On reflection, she never would ask that. She respects the privacy of the individual too much. She's an admirable woman, my mother, she truly is. She's a rock, dependable, always there when you need her.

'Got any homework?' she asked.

'Yes. French. Thought I'd get it over and done with so that I can enjoy the weekend.'

'Good idea. If you need any help . . .?'

'Thanks.'

She picked up a book from a chair in the hall and went on up the stairs to the drawing room. I felt sorry for her as I watched her go. It was the first time that I'd ever felt sorry for my mother and it frightened me.

I hadn't had time to go upstairs before the doorbell rang. It couldn't be *her*, could it? I hastened to the door and opened it to find Mark on the step.

'Wondered if you'd fancy a game of tennis?'

'It's a bit late for that.'

'Or chess?' He grinned. He's a whizz at chess, goes in for competitions, and has been teaching me to play.

'OK,' I said and in he came.

'Who is it, dear?' came my mother's voice from above.

'Mark. We're going to play chess.'

'Fine. Hello, Mark,' she called over the banister rail.

'Hello, Mrs Malone,' he called back up politely. 'How are you?'

'Very well, thank you.'

My mother would be pleased to see me going into the kitchen to play chess with Mark. She knew his mother. They were at school together. That's what Edinburgh is like, or certain sections of it. You can't go far without bumping into someone who knows someone else that you know.

I fetched us a couple of Cokes from the larder and Mark and I settled in to play chess. I was improving, slowly. He was a patient teacher. I was glad to be doing something that absorbed me and took me away from my preoccupation for a while.

Dad came in in the middle of our game and he also was happy to see Mark and greeted him in a friendly fashion. Both my parents liked him. He's an uncomplicated sort of guy with an open face and an easy smile. I like him as well, but not as he would wish. I think of him more as another brother, but he doesn't see me as a sister.

Before leaving he asked if I'd like to go to the cinema the following day. With relatives on my mother's side visiting all weekend, I wouldn't even have a chance to see Charlotte, and I'd already decided to see Eve on Monday, so I suggested Tuesday and said we could ask Charlotte and Donald to join us. Mark's face clouded over.

'I thought we might go on our own for a change.'

'Trouble is, I promised Charlie I'd see her on Tuesday.' I hadn't, but again I told myself it was only another white lie, for Charlotte and I often did go out during the week.

These little white lies were beginning to pile up!

Chapter 10

On the Monday, as soon as Dad had dropped us off at school, I told Charlotte we were booked for the cinema on Tuesday evening. She wasn't free, she said. She was going to a concert with her parents. Everything seemed to be going criss-cross at the moment as if the stars – *my* stars – were clashing in their courses.

'We can let the boys know later,' said Charlotte. 'You could always come to the concert with us?'

'Mmm, maybe. Oh, by the way, I can't do anything after school today.'

'Don't tell me you're going to visit your Aunt Etta *again*!'

'No, of course not.'

'What are you up to then? Emmie, you're not seeing someone on the quiet, are you, and not telling me?'

'Don't be silly! Who would I be seeing?'

I went home after school and changed into my oldest pair of jeans (which my mother was threatening to bin) and a faded emerald green sweatshirt. I wasn't going to look like Little Miss Goody-Two-Shoes out at the caravan site in my school uniform again. Then I made up my eyes, using green eyeliner and long-lash black mascara.

I considered cycling out there, but it was quite a way and I didn't fancy the traffic, so I walked up to Princes Street and caught a bus. My stomach was doing a few flips on the way out. Charlotte, if she knew, would think I was nuts to be doing what I was doing. The cautious side of me thought the same thing but I desperately wanted to go. I hated my shadow for what she was doing to us but, on the other hand, I was drawn to her, like metal to a magnet.

It was a great relief, however, to arrive at the site and find that Lenny and Jason were absent.

'They're in Edinburgh,' said Eve. 'Working.'

Begging, I presumed.

'Hey, you're looking great! It's good you came.' She smiled. 'I knew you would. Fancy a beer?'

'Sure.'

'Lager OK?' She took two cans from the fridge and poured them into white plastic tumblers. She raised hers to me. 'Here's to sisterhood!'

I didn't repeat the words, but I drank.

'Nicked by Naughty Lenny, I'm afraid.' She held up one of the cans. 'Doesn't bother you, does it, drinking nicked beer?'

'Not as long as I didn't nick it myself.'

She laughed.

'You're my sister and I don't even know what kind of things turn you on,' she said. 'Leaving out tennis and drinking cappuccinos. God. How can you stand all that milky stuff! What kind of music do you like?'

'Folk. Reggae. Jazz.'

'You like jazz? Fantastic! So do I. Fancy, we've got something in common! Not too surprising, I guess. We must have a lot of the same genes inside us. I had a boyfriend once who was a sax player. That was what turned me on to jazz. I became a jazz groupie.'

What age could she have been when she got into that? We talked about jazz and drank our lager and when we'd finished the first two cans she produced two more.

'What else do you like?' I asked her.

'I read,' she told me. 'Books. Does that surprise you? My mum was a great reader. Never away from the library.' She lifted *Trainspotting* down from a shelf. 'Thought I'd get clued up on Edinburgh. Ain't seen much of that side, at least, not yet.'

'There are a lot of different sides to the city.'

'You said that very primly.'

'Did I?' Then I giggled and so did she and we ended up in one of those laughing fits which you have to bring to an end when your stomach starts to ache.

'I've read *The Prime of Miss Jean Brodie* too,' said Eve when we'd calmed down. 'Is your school like that?'

'No, mine's even posher,' I said, and we started to giggle again.

She brought out two more cans of lager.

'This is the last for me,' I said, lifting my tumbler.

'Ain't got any more. Not till Lenny comes back. Don't worry, he'll be a while yet. He'll hang in till he catches the people going home from work.'

'How do you feel when you're begging?'

'Like dirt. I don't do it much. Did some busking in London, me and my previous boyfriend.'

'The sax player?'

'No, this one played the guitar, well, sort of. He was a twanger.'

That set us off laughing again.

I suddenly looked at my watch and saw what the time was. My mother would already be home and I had a long bus ride to get back.

'Must you go? Already?'

'Afraid so.'

'You don't have much freedom, do you, Emily?' Eve had that taunting note back in her voice again. One minute I liked her, the next I didn't.

'I wouldn't say that.'

'Don't go all huffy on me! Bet you've got to be in by ten every night?'

'Not every night.'

'Why don't you come out with me one night? We could have a girls' night out. A sisters' night out.'

'I'll see.'

'You'll come again though, won't you?'

'I guess so.'

'Good.' She grinned.

She saw me off again from the door of the van. I looked back to wave, then I made my way a trifle unsteadily back to the main road. Walking away I realised I hadn't even mentioned the idea of her leaving Edinburgh, let alone done anything to persuade her. When I reached the bus stop I realised that I was desperate to go to the loo. I'd just drunk three lagers after all! Three! On an empty stomach. No wonder I felt a bit light-headed. And my bladder felt fit to burst. I had to find some bushes. I walked along the road till I found a thick enough clump. While I was squatting there I heard a bus arrive and leave again.

If there'd been a handy phone box I'd have called my mother to say I was going to be late, but of course when you want one there isn't one. Sod's law. That being so, there's a lot to be said for mobile phones, but my mother dislikes them except for use in emergencies. She says we don't know yet whether or not they carry health risks so she won't allow me to have one though half the girls in school tote them around. They're to be seen – and heard – in the playground conducting the most rubbishy conversations you've ever had to listen to.

I had to wait twenty minutes before another bus came. I clambered thankfully on board. Before going home I'd have to buy myself some strong mints to mask the smell on my breath.

On the way back into town, I thought of the time I'd just spent with Eve. I found her past life incredible. She'd done so much and there she was, the same age as me! My life, in comparison, seemed stuffy and hemmed in, though I wouldn't have admitted it to her.

I suppose if it hadn't been for Eve (and my intake of lager) I wouldn't have let Greg pick me up on the top deck of a bus. I'd never done such a thing before.

Part way into town this guy wearing dark-blue overalls got on and sat beside me. I didn't even look at his face. I moved over so that he wouldn't squash me, but when the bus took a wide bend he swung over almost on top of me.

'Sorry about that,' he said, moving back.

'That's all right,' I said.

Then I looked at him. He had the most wonderful dark-brown eyes I'd ever seen and he was smiling at me.

Chapter 11

We got talking on the bus. He told me he was a motor mechanic and he'd just come from a job. He'd been delivering a car and hadn't had the chance to get changed. He showed me the grease on his hands apologetically. He ran a car of his own, a bit of an old banger, but it was off the road at present. It needed a new fan belt. He was eighteen years old. I told him I was still at school, but not which school, and that I was sixteen (well, I was in my sixteenth year and I thought fifteen might seem a bit young to him). It's amazing how in a few stops on a bus ride you can fill in the basic details about yourself.

We both got off at the same stop on Princes Street.

He said, 'Would you like to go for a drink?'

I said, 'I think I could do with a cup of coffee. And maybe something to eat. I've just drunk three lagers.'

'That's pretty good going for an afternoon's drinking.'

'I don't usually drink that much in an afternoon.'

'No, you don't look as if you do,' he said, taking my arm and steadying me. 'Where would you like to go?'

'What about Henderson's?' I said.

He didn't know it. It was a vegetarian restaurant and wine bar, an Edinburgh institution where I knew I could get coffee and food and he could have whatever he wanted.

'Hanover Street,' I said.

'Fine.'

He led me there and placed me at a table while he queued up. He brought back a tray bearing coffee, a bottle of mineral water, a glass of beer (for himself) and some oatcakes and cheese.

'You get cracking on these,' he said, putting the coffee and oatcakes in front of me. 'I'm going to take off these overalls.'

I drank the coffee and started on the oatcakes and immediately began to feel less woozy. Greg came back with clean hands and wearing a blue T-shirt and jeans and for a minute I didn't recognise him.

'I liked you in your overalls,' I told him.

'You're kidding! In that case, I'd have kept them on. Drink that water now! And eat the cheese!'

I did as he told me. He drank his beer and now that he was sitting opposite me I had the chance to study him properly. In the bus, sitting side by side, I hadn't had a clear view of him. He was gorgeous! I'd better not tell him so, I thought, and in the next minute I did and he laughed, throwing his head back.

'You're pretty gorgeous yourself!'

'Really?'

'And you're just a little bit drunk.'

'Not so drunk I can't see you,' I said, and he laughed again.

When I had sobered up quite a bit more I thought of my mother who would be wondering where I was and phoning everybody she could think of to ask if they had seen me.

'I'll have to go,' I said reluctantly. I would so much rather have stayed.

'I'll see you home. Where do you live?'

'Stockbridge.' It was a vague enough answer.

We set off down the hill and after a moment he put his arm round my waist, which felt very comfortable, so I did not resist. When we reached the bridge at Stockbridge I brought him to a halt.

'You needn't come the rest of the way.'

'Why not? Which is your street?'

When I told him he dropped his arm. Our street is reckoned to be one of the most expensive in Edinburgh.

'I see.'

'I wouldn't mind you seeing me home but my parents –'

'Wouldn't like you to be seen with me?'

'No, no, honestly, it's not that! It's just they'd wonder –'

'I understand.'

We stood apart and I felt miserable. 'I'd like to see you again, Greg, really I would. Can I give you my phone number?'

He nodded and I wrote it on a scrap of paper I found in my bag.

'Thanks for looking after me,' I said.

'It was a pleasure!'

And so we parted. I went up the hill to our house feeling elated and miserable at the same time. I'd just met the first guy who'd really turned me on but I was racked by anxiety thinking that he might back off and not phone because he thought I came from a different world from him.

I opened our front door apprehensively, calling out, 'It's me, I'm back.' It was half past eight. There was no response. I went on into the kitchen and found a note on the table saying, '7 p.m. Where have you been? We're off to the Lyceum. Dinner in fridge ready to pop into microwave. Should be back by 10. Love, Mum.'

Thank goodness they'd been going to the theatre! I put my meal into the microwave but could eat only half of it so scraped the rest down the loo and flushed it away. I was dying to talk to someone about Greg, but it was out of the question to tell Charlotte. *You mean you let this guy pick you up on the bus?*

When the phone rang I nearly jumped out of my skin. But it wasn't Greg. It was silly of me, anyway, to think he'd phone this evening. We'd just parted, after all.

'Oh, hi, Mark,' I said.

He said that as Charlotte wasn't free on Tuesday, what about still going to the cinema, just he and I? I said I was sorry but I didn't think I could make it.

'You don't want to, is that what you mean?'

'I'm sorry, Mark.'

He put the receiver down.

It rang again five minutes later and this time it was Charlotte who wanted a chat. I had nothing to chat about fit for her ears, so after a few minutes the conversation more or less dried up and she rang off less than thrilled with me. Oh well, could I help it?

The next time it rang, it was my sister.

'Eve,' I said, 'you'll never guess, but coming home on the bus I met this guy . . .' I told her everything I knew about him, which was not a great deal.

'Go for him!' she told me.

'How can I go for him? I don't know where he lives, where he works.' And I was becoming convinced that he wouldn't phone. I sat gazing at the stupid machine for the next hour, but it didn't emit a single sound.

My parents came in just after ten and I made up a story about why I'd been late home. I'd gone to visit a girl in my class who lived halfway to Glasgow and I'd missed a bus . . . My mother naturally had to ask who she was so I told her the name of a girl who did live out there though she and I were not particular friends. My father seemed to believe me, but I didn't think my mother did. I went to bed.

After school next day I didn't dare spurn Charlotte again, so I asked her to come home for a coffee before she went to the concert. I wanted to be in the house, anyway, in case Greg called.

We had coffee and nobody rang and Charlotte eventually went home and then my mother came in and after that my father, who was not working late for once, and we settled down to a family meal.

'You really are off your food, aren't you?' said my mother.

The phone rang and I jumped up, knocking the table against their knees.

'Steady,' said my father, holding on to the edge of it. 'It can't be that important, can it?'

I was already out of the door and making for the phone. I almost dropped the receiver.

'Hi,' he said, 'it's Greg. Remember me?'

'Of course!'

'I wasn't sure whether to ring you.'

'I'm glad you did.'

'Really?'

'Yes, really.'

'Good. When can I see you?'

'When would you like to see me?'

'What about now?'

'Give me half an hour.'

'I could wait that long. Just. Where shall I see you?'

'On the bridge at Stockbridge.'

I went back to the dining room, but stayed on the threshold.

'Who was it?' asked my mother.

'A friend. I'm going out now, just for a couple of hours.'

'I see.'

'Won't be late.'

I closed the door and raced upstairs to change into my best pair of trousers and a purple shirt. I put purple liner on my eyes and long-lash mascara on my eyelashes and pinky-purple lipstick on my lips. Behind my ears I smeared perfume given to me by Charlotte for Christmas. It was evening and the air would be cooling, so I threw a light cream jacket round my shoulders and then I was ready.

My parents were emerging from the dining room as I descended the stairs. They seemed taken aback by the sight of me. They said nothing.

I said, 'See you later,' and then I was outside, flying along the street as if my feet were winged.

I was five minutes early but he was already there. I went straight into his arms as if I had met him a dozen times before. We met with a kiss which went on and on and obliterated the rest of the world and even when we drew back for a minute we had to kiss again. I scarcely registered Charlotte's father uttering my name in a slightly shocked tone. I thought, *There goes Mr McDowell. Too bad!* I saw him pass and look round as if he was trying to check that his eyes were not betraying him. I didn't care, not one bit. I was more interested in Greg than Charlotte's father.

Entwined, we walked the streets of Edinburgh that night, finding out about each other. His dad was dead, he lived with his mother and younger sister in a flat in Tollcross. He'd left school at sixteen: he'd had no other option. They needed the money. His dream was to have a garage of his own but he said he'd need to win the Lottery first. I told him about my family and said, 'Don't be put off by them.'

I let him walk me to my gate this time. He looked at our house and I said, 'It's only a house. My dad grew up in a tenement in Leith.'

It was almost midnight. We stood there, reluctant to part. We kissed again. There were lights on inside the house.

'I'd better go,' I said as a church clock struck twelve.

'Cinderella,' he said, smoothing back my hair.

'You know where to come if I drop my glass slipper.'

We kissed a final goodnight.

'See you tomorrow?'

I nodded.

I opened the gate and went up the path. He waited until I was opening the door. I blew a kiss back down the path at him and then I went inside to face the music.

'Emily, do you know what the time is?'

'Of course I do! I've been able to tell the time for a while now.'

My parents were not in the mood to be amused.

'You have school in the morning.'

'I know that too.'

'Have you done your homework?'

'Most of it.'

'Who is this boy?'

'Which boy?'

'The one you were out with.'

'He's called Greg. Short for Gregory. After Peck. His mother was a fan.'

'Emily, have you been drinking?'

'Not a drop.'

'He's not one of the boys in the group that you know, is he?'

'Greg? No, thank goodness for that. He's a motor mechanic.'

That took their breath away and allowed me to escape and go to my bed to sleep, perchance to dream.

Chapter 12

The atmosphere at breakfast was tense, but since I never sit down for more than five minutes in the morning, just enough time to eat a slice of wholemeal toast and swallow a cup of tea, I didn't have to endure it for long. My mother was frowning and my father looking uncomfortable as he tried to pretend that he was reading the business section of the *Scotsman*.

As I was about to leave the room my mother called me back. 'Just a minute, Emily!'

'Yes?'

'You know very well we have a rule that on week nights you are to be home by ten o'clock, unless there is a special reason.'

'Last night was special.'

'Where did you meet this boy?'

'On a bus.'

'On a *bus*? Have you taken leave of your senses? You let a stranger, someone you knew absolutely nothing about, pick you up on a bus?'

'Yes.'

My mother was now looking expectantly at my father, waiting for him to come in. He said in a quiet voice, 'That could be rather dangerous, Emily.'

I couldn't resist smiling. I felt like living dangerously for a change.

'Are you seeing him again?' asked my mother.

I said I was seeing him that very evening.

'Why don't you bring him home so that we can meet him?'

'I don't want him to be interrogated.'

My father cleared his throat. 'Perhaps if we promised not to?'

'Not tonight,' I said and made to open the door. I wanted to keep him to myself for a while, before I would even toy with the idea of exposing him to my family, or to Charlotte.

'Emily!' My mother stopped me again. 'Ten o'clock this evening, and no later, you understand?'

I didn't answer. I thought it unlikely I would be ready to come home at ten. What could she do to me if I stayed out till eleven? Throw me out of the house? She wouldn't do that. Lock me in my room the next night? I'd climb down the drainpipe. Stop my allowance? That would seem to be her only feasible sanction but, if she did, I had a thousand pounds in the building society, didn't I?

On the short journey to pick up Charlotte my father said, 'You seem to be rather keen on this young man, Emily.'

'I am. You know how it is, Dad, sometimes you just meet someone and you take to them straight away.'

He said nothing for a moment. Was he thinking of Eve's mother? Then he cautioned me. 'You must be careful, though. When you're carried away your judgement can be a bit warped.'

'He's nice, Dad. You'd like him.'

'I'd like to meet him.'

We were outside the McDowells' house. Dad tooted his horn and their front door opened and out came Charlotte with her mother right behind her. Mrs McDowell usually stayed on the step to watch us depart but today she followed Charlotte down the path on to the pavement. She was wearing lavender-blue furry slippers. I'd have thought she would have considered it to be a bit off to go out in the street in slippers.

'Good morning, John,' she said to my father, but it was me she was eyeing.

'Looks like being a good day,' responded my father.

'And how are you this morning, Emily?'

'Very well, thank you, Mrs McDowell.' I gave her a big smile.

Charlotte had by now managed to get herself and her belongings into the back seat and my father was starting the engine. We waved goodbye to Mrs McDowell, who stood there to watch us go, lavender-blue feet astride, her hands parked on either side of her hips.

Of course, Charlotte was agog to ask me ten million questions and as soon as we'd slammed the car doors behind us she was off. 'So you *are* seeing someone and you didn't tell me! That's mean. I tell you everything. Who is he, the guy Dad saw you with?'

'He's called Greg.'

'Greg what?'

'I don't know.' I'd not thought to ask. Surnames were unimportant anyway.

'Where does he live?'

'A flat at Tollcross. He lives with his mother and sister.'

'What do they do?'

'His sister's at school and his mother's an office cleaner.'

'An office cleaner?' I'd taken Charlotte's breath away.

'What's wrong with that? It's good honest work.'

'I never said it wasn't. Is he still at school?'

'Course not. He's eighteen. He's a motor mechanic and he loves his job.'

She then had to find out where I'd met him and all of that. I enjoyed recounting it. I could have gone over the details for ever.

'Is he good looking?'

'Charlie, he's gorgeous!'

'He certainly sounds very, well, *different*.'

'You can say that again!'

'But what do you have in common?'

'Sex!'

'Emmie, you've not?'

'*No*, not *yet*.' I love winding Charlotte up.

'Not *yet*? You've only known him a couple of days.'

'It feels like a long, long time,' I said dreamily. The bell was ringing and it was time to go in, but I didn't feel like sitting all day in a classroom bending my mind to things like physics and French. I wanted to have room in my head to think about Greg. I considered for a moment turning tail and not going in, but decided against it. That would cause too much furore both in school and at home. I thought of Eve in her caravan free to do what she wanted all day and I envied her.

'Emmie, I think you've gone mad!' declared Charlotte as we tagged on to the back of the line.

I smiled. Madness had much to commend it.

The day in school seemed endless. I kept looking at my watch. The second hand was lumbering with maddening slowness round the face. I wrote his name on the inside back cover of my English jotter. GREG. Then I wrote my own. EMILY. Greg and Emily. Emily and Greg. I drew a circle around them. A charmed circle. Or so I hoped. Charlotte leaned over to see what I was writing and made a face at me. She passed a note. 'You are off your rocker!' I passed a note back. 'It's bliss being off your rocker. It's like orbiting into space. I recommend it.' The English teacher interceded at this point and demanded to have my note. Charlotte handed it over. The teacher read it, silently, and shook her head at both of us. I was ticked off in two further classes for not paying attention and when it came to handing in our French homework I only then remembered that I had not done it. Another ticking off and a promise on my part to bring it in without fail the next day. When the final bell went I felt like cheering.

I didn't have a problem with Charlotte that afternoon as she had another music lesson.

'I could come round this evening,' she suggested.

'I'm seeing Greg,' I said and couldn't keep the smile off my face.

'What about tomorrow?'

'Can't promise.'

'Is your mother going to let you go out with him *every* night?'

'It's not up to her, is it? She can hardly chain me to the bedpost.'

Charlotte went off annoyed with me yet again, but I couldn't help that. I was going to go and visit Eve. She was the one person I knew who would understand and be sympathetic. She wouldn't be judgemental. The trouble with Charlotte was that her vision of life was too narrow. The height of excitement for her was to go to the cinema in a foursome with Donald and Mark.

I went home to change. I was in the middle of putting on my eyeshadow when the phone rang. I had a feeling it might be him! I ran to the nearest phone, which was in my parents' bedroom.

'Hi!' I said.

'So you're home, Emily,' said my mother. 'Good. I hope you'll be getting down to your homework. Perhaps you could do the veg for tonight's meal? There's a cauliflower in the fridge and some carrots in the veg basket.'

'Oh, Mum,' I wailed. 'I was just going out for an hour. I've been in school all day and I've got a headache.'

'You can do your homework outside if you clean off the white garden table. That'll give you some fresh air. Make sure you wipe the table carefully so that you don't get any marks on your books. And take an aspirin for your headache if it doesn't go away.'

I made a face at the wall. I knew what she was up to, trying to keep me chained to the house. It was a wonder she didn't want me to weed the garden as well and do a spot of ironing. When she'd rung off I went down to the kitchen and scraped the carrots at great speed under the tap and stuck them in a pot of cold water, then I hacked the cauliflower into pieces, rinsed them and left them in a colander. Chores done, I grabbed my French homework – I was planning to do it on the bus – and stuffed it into a carrier bag and finally let myself out of the house.

Before going for the bus on Princes Street I had another call to make. At the building society where all my worldly wealth is lodged. I was going to draw out fifty pounds and give it to Eve to keep her going and so that she wouldn't have to sit at the foot of the Playfair Steps and beg. I took my savings book out of my bag and joined the queue. When I reached the counter I said I'd like to draw out some money and the woman slid a form across to me. I filled it out, putting down my name and so forth. There was also a box for date of birth. I passed the slip back along with my bank book. The woman looked at the form and then at me.

'I'm afraid you'll need a parent's signature. You're under age.'

'Oh,' I said. 'What age do you have to be not to need a parent's signature?'

'Sixteen.'

'Sixteen,' I repeated. 'Fine.'

'Either your mother or father will do.' She returned to me both the book and the withdrawal form.

I put the book in my bag and dropped the withdrawal form into the nearest litter bin. So much for that. It was as well Eve hadn't said she'd take the thousand pounds and disappear.

On the ride going out of town I managed to do a few sentences of the homework, though the writing, I had to confess, was not of my neatest and might not pass muster. The trouble was that the bus swayed a lot and sometimes braked abruptly at lights and when it started again it lurched. Once we'd left the busy part of town behind it ran more smoothly and I managed to do another few lines. But I really needed a French dictionary, so I put the books away and just looked out of the window.

I was up on my feet and down the stairs as soon as I saw the terminus coming up. I was the only person left on the bus. I leaped off and crossed the road.

There was a man sweeping the paths at the caravan park. He glanced up and muttered, 'Hi, Eve!' It wasn't a very warm greeting, but it made me smile because he had mistaken me for Eve! I thought he might be the manager, for Eve had said he was a one-man band and did everything himself. It seemed that he wasn't too fond of his tenants in the old van beside the back hedge. Eve said he'd complained a couple of times about them playing loud music but she'd said to him, 'Who's to hear? The place is as dead as a dodo.'

I was halfway through the park when I realised I'd forgotten my carrier bag. I'd left it on the bus! I raced back – the bus would have to wait for a minute or two before returning to town. I was just in time to see it taking off. I waved frantically at the driver but he paid no attention. He stared ahead and went on his way, damn him!

I returned to the caravan park. At the entrance stood an extra-long van with the word RECEPTION above the door. This was where the manager lived. He was at the window and he was the same man I'd seen brushing the path. He gave me an odd look, I thought. Maybe he was wondering if I *was* Eve, after all.

Her caravan door was closed. Had I come all this way to find she was out? Hadn't I said I'd probably see her today? I rapped on the door and called her name. For a moment I thought I was totally out of luck, then I heard a movement inside.

The door opened and Lenny stuck his head round.

'Oh, it's you, Miss Emily!'

I took a step back. 'Is Eve in?' I asked.

'She'll be back any time. She's gone to do an errand.' He opened the door wide. 'But come in, do! Come into my parlour!'

Said the spider to a fly.

I was a fool to go in, but I did.

Chapter 13

Lenny pulled the door shut behind me. As soon as he did I felt on the verge of panic, but I took a deep breath and told myself to calm down. Panicking wouldn't help. And he was probably harmless. Well, so I tried to tell myself.

'It's a bit stuffy in here, isn't it?' I said.

'There's a cold wind blowing out there. There always is. It's like Siberia. Grrr. And I've got trouble with my chest.' He gave a croaking cough as if to prove it and spat a gobbet of phlegm into a grimy rag. 'That's why I'm not working today. I have a delicate chest.' He grinned at me. 'What's your chest like? Is it delicate?'

I didn't answer but I don't think he expected one. I was already wondering how to escape. Jason was in the van, lying stretched full length on one of the side seats, snoring his head off. I was worried that if I tried to leave Lenny might set the dog on me and although he had only four teeth I feared they could do enough damage. What an idiot I'd been to come in in the first place! My best bet was to try to humour Lenny and hope that Eve wouldn't be long.

'You might be better in a warmer climate,' I said. 'For your chest.'

'Expect we'll move on one of these days.'

'Where do you think you might go?'

'Who can tell? Florida. South of France. You could come with us! How's about that, eh?'

I tried to smile.

'Hey, come on, Miss Emily, don't just stand there, sit down! Take a pew! We're civilised here. We've got seats.

Hey, you, Jason, get your bloody carcass off of there!' He cuffed the dog's ear, which made the animal open one eye, but he seemed to get the message, because he slid down off the bench and crawled underneath. 'Knows his master, does Jason.'

Lenny then invited me to sit on the seat the dog had just vacated. 'One minute though!' he cried and he scrabbled underneath the tiny sink and produced another greyish rag with which he proceeded to clean the bench, making a great play of it. 'Fit for a queen's rear now!' He held out his hand. 'Madam, your throne awaits you!'

I sat down on the edge.

'Sit back, relax! Don't be so bloody uptight. I won't let Jason bite, will I, Jason?'

Jason yawned. I heard, though I didn't see it, for he was lying underneath my seat now and he smelt as badly, if not worse, than on that first day I'd come here. Then, Eve had kept the door open. She'd said she didn't like it shut. Being in tightly enclosed spaces gave her claustrophobia. That was another thing we had in common.

There was a big window straight ahead of me, on the opposite wall of the van, and one right behind my back. Looking out front, I could see only the high privet hedge that marked the boundary of the campsite. Twisting round, I saw through the back window that a van was parked parallel to this one. The door was shut and the curtains were closed. Nobody was at home, obviously.

'What can I get you, madam?' asked Lenny. 'Can of lager? Eve said you like lager.'

I didn't like the idea that Eve had been discussing me with him, but of course she would. She *lived* with him, didn't she? How could she? It's known to be a mystery why some people fancy each other, but there are limits, aren't there? I would have thought Lenny would be off limits for anyone.

He was holding aloft a can of lager. I'd rather have had a coffee or a glass of water or nothing, but since I was trying to humour him I thought it might be a good idea to go along with what he was offering, as far as possible. Also, if I had something to drink out of a can then he couldn't put anything in it. Did I think he might have tried to? I didn't know, that was the problem. I didn't know how to assess him, how his mind might work. Slyly, I thought. Everything about him suggested slyness. I was on tenterhooks and he was enjoying it.

He zipped open the can and presented it to me with a flourish. It seemed I was not going to be given anything to drink out of and I was not going to ask. I had no intention of drinking very much, I didn't want to get into the state I'd been in on Monday. I raised the can to my lips and let a little of the lager dribble out of the jagged hole into my mouth. More went slithering down my chin to my neck than went into my mouth and I had to rummage for a tissue, which amused Lenny. Whatever I did seemed to amuse him.

'Like this,' he said, tipping his head right back. The lager glugged into his throat and his hairy Adam's apple moved up and down. He jerked his head upright again. 'Go on, you can do it!'

'I'll do it my own way,' I said.

'Great! I love a woman who knows her own mind. Don't want to be told what to do by a poor sod of a man, do you?' He brought his leering face down close to mine and I had to stretch my neck back to avoid him. His breath smelt almost as foul as the dog's. He grinned and jumped back up.

'I must be going soon,' I said.

'Can't let you do that. Not before Eve comes back. She'd be angry with me if I let you go. And let me tell you when Eve gets angry you don't want to be around.'

'Has she got a hot temper?' *Keep him talking*, I told myself. *Talk about Eve. Deflect him from yourself.*

'You could say that. She goes up like a rocket. Comes down again quite fast though. Quick to go up, quick to come down. Zoom! Not like me. I operate on a slow fuse.'

That didn't do much to reassure me. My throat felt parched so I lifted the can and let another few drops trickle into my mouth. Lenny had taken a joint from a shelf and lit it, adding yet another smell to the little room.

'Does she lose her temper often?' I asked, desperately searching for other topics of conversation and not finding any. My mind felt frozen.

'Eve? Naw, not too often. Not more than once an hour. Want a drag?' He offered me the joint and I shook my head, saying I'd stick with the lager. 'Go on, don't be so bloody scared!'

'I'm not scared!' My own temper boiled up, fuelled by the horrible thought of having to put anything in my mouth that he had had in his. 'I just don't want it, can't you understand that?'

'Wowee, fantastic! I love it when your eyes spark. Like glowing coals, they are.'

I simmered down. 'I don't know if I can wait for Eve.'

'Yes, you can. You know, she's got a great imagination, has your sister. You don't want to believe everything she tells you.'

'No?'

'No.' He shook his head.

'It's too hot in here for me,' I had to say eventually. 'It's making me feel ill.' I wiped the sweat from my forehead with the back of my hand. My hands were wet too. I dried them off on my jeans. 'Can we have the door open?'

'Can't stand open doors. Make me nervous.' He wriggled his fingers. On three on his right hand he wore heavy square-shaped rings. Knuckledusters? I didn't know. My experience was way behind my half-sister's.

'Anyone could walk in,' he was saying. 'Know what I mean? But I wouldn't like you to be ill, Miss Emily. I'll open the window, that should do the trick.'

He opened the opposite window as wide as it would go and I felt a rush of cool air, which helped as far as temperature was concerned. Also, I thought, if I had to scream for help, someone might hear me. But who? The manager was in his van at the other end of the site, unless he'd come out to do some more chores. If I'd thought he was anywhere near by I might have tried to make a run for it, but Lenny had stayed on his feet the whole time and was between me and the door. I wouldn't get far. Not even as far as the door. There was nothing else to do but sit it out and stay cool. Stay *cool*? Fat chance of that. Eve *must* come back soon.

'Where *is* Eve?' I asked.

'Making a delivery. Said she might call on her aunt afterwards. *Your* aunt.'

So Eve might be sitting in Aunt Etta's warm, cosy kitchen, drinking tea and eating bacon rolls and feeling too soporific to stir herself and come home.

'Look, Lenny,' I said, trying to sound pleasant, 'I think I really should be going. I'm expected home.'

'But we're just getting to know each other!' He dropped down on to the bench beside me. I moved away but there wasn't much room for manoeuvre. 'You're not afraid of me, are you?' he asked softly. Of course I was and he knew it. I was petrified. He took another drag on his joint and leaned back with his eyes closed but only for a moment. He looked sideways at me. 'Relax. You're jumpy, aren't you? But I ain't planning to hurt you.'

Maybe he wasn't. Maybe I was misreading his signals, though I didn't think so. I wasn't that naive. The one thing I knew was that I had to get out of there. I half rose, but he put out an arm and eased me back on to the seat. 'I'll let you go when I'm good and ready,' he said.

I'd had enough of being passive, waiting for him to make the next move. 'I'm going!' I cried, and tried to get up again. This time he seized my arm and held it fast.

'You're hurting me! You said you wouldn't.'

'I won't hurt you if you behave yourself, Miss Emily. So why don't you just stop struggling? It's not going to get you anywhere, is it? Nowhere at all.'

He was twisting my arm. I felt pain shoot right up into my shoulder blade. I couldn't help but cry out. I let myself go limp.

'That's better. Much better. That's a good little girl now. Wants to be nice to her Uncle Lenny, doesn't she? Course she does.' He had slackened his grip on my arm, but now he reached out with his other hand and began to stroke my hair. The touch of his fingers made my flesh crawl. 'You're pretty. Very pretty. Like Eve. You're a dead ringer for each other. I never expected to have two of you. You could say you're a bonus. It's like winning the Lottery.'

His face was close to mine now. I saw the spittle lying on his half-open lips. I felt his breath on my mouth.

'*Please*,' I whispered.

At that moment I heard a faint noise outside the van. Somebody or something was moving.

'Eve!' I screamed.

'Shut your gob!' He slammed his hand over my mouth.

Suddenly, there came a bang on the door and a loud male voice shouted, 'Open up! Police!'

Chapter 14

I thought the police had come to rescue me but they hadn't. They'd come on a raid. They were looking for drugs.

There were five of them out there, three constables in uniform, one of whom was a woman, and two men in plain clothes, one built like a boxer, the other thin with a razor-sharp face. I'd seen enough TV police dramas to guess that the two in plain clothes were detectives, but I wasn't yet aware that they were from the drug squad.

I broke away from Lenny and stumbled to the door. 'Thank goodness you've come! I didn't know what I was going to do. He was molesting me, he was going to –' I couldn't go on, I was trembling too much.

'*Molesting* her?' said a voice in the background. I saw that it belonged to the park manager, who was standing at the back of the police group. 'Load of old cobblers. They've been living together in there for the last three weeks. She's no angel.'

'I don't live here,' I said desperately. 'I was just visiting.'

'I've heard that one before,' said one of the male constables.

'But I was!'

'We'll have you out then,' said the heavily built detective. 'And anybody else that's still in there.'

I jumped out eagerly and immediately the woman constable came forward and produced a pair of handcuffs! I couldn't believe my eyes. They were going to arrest me!

'I haven't done anything, I tell you. I'm not Eve, the girl who's been living in there. My name's Emily.'

'We'll get all that sorted out in a minute,' said the woman, clipping on the handcuffs and joining my wrist to hers. 'Meantime, we want to be sure that you don't get any ideas in your head.'

Did she mean, try to escape? How could I with five police in the offing? This was turning into another nightmare, of a different kind.

'Right, come on you!' said the detective to Lenny, who was still lounging on the seat inside the caravan. Jason was sitting between his feet with his tongue hanging out and looking more alert than I'd yet seen him. 'And you needn't think the dog's going to protect you. If you know what's good for you you'll come quietly.' The man made a move up the steps and at that Lenny rose, but taking his time.

'Keep cool, man. I never said I wouldn't come, did I?'

'You'll be having plenty of time to cool off! Get out of there! And bring the dog with you.'

The two male constables came forward, one with handcuffs for Lenny, the other with a chain and a muzzle for the dog.

'Jason never bit anybody in his life!' protested Lenny.

'We're making certain he won't get the chance to.'

Lenny looked at the site manager. 'So it was you what shopped us, was it? *Scum!*' He spat at the man, who drew back just in time, and the constable linked to Lenny pulled him away.

The two detectives now entered the van and began to take the place apart. It was only then that it clicked in my stupid head that they were searching for drugs.

'Can you confirm that these two people have been renting this van on your site for the past three weeks?' the policewoman asked the manager.

He could, he said. He pointed first at Lenny, 'His name's Lenny Smith, believe that if you like. The girl's called Eve Malone.'

'I'm *not*! My name's Emily, I tell you!'

'Emily what?' asked the policewoman.

'Malone. But there are two of us, really there are.'

'Twins?' She didn't believe me, anyway.

'No. Sisters. Well, half-sisters.'

'Her name's Eve,' put in Lenny. 'She's just making it up. She's got too much imagination, haven't you, luv? Fancy saying I was trying to molest you! That wasn't very nice, was it?' He grinned at me.

'I'm not making anything up.' I appealed to the policewoman attached to my arm. 'I never have lived here, I swear I haven't.'

'She's lived here right beside me,' said Lenny. 'Snug as two bugs in a rug we've been.'

'Don't believe him! He's lying!'

'So where do you claim to have been living?' asked the policewoman.

I named my street.

'Oh, aye. Well, Emily or Eve, whichever you prefer, we'll check that out when we get down to the station.'

I didn't say at this point that my mother was a lawyer. My *mother*! I hadn't given her a thought so far. Or my father. I presumed they would be summoned to the police station. They'd have to be before I'd be released. And then all the cats would be well and truly out of the bag and yowling their heads off.

I glanced over my shoulder and gasped. Eve was standing down by the entrance gate.

'There she is!' I cried, turning back to the constables. 'Eve! Down by the gate.'

They all wheeled around to look and I might have been able to predict that there would be nobody there. Eve had done *another* of her vanishing tricks.

'I saw her. Honestly, I did!' I felt like bursting into tears, but I was determined not to break down in front of Lenny. He'd enjoy that. I'd never met an out-and-out sadist before.

The constable with the dog said he'd take a look and off he went at a jog through the site, forcing Jason to keep up. Meanwhile the detectives were making a racket in their ripping apart of the caravan, and bits and pieces had been tossed out on to the grass and the manager was starting to protest. It was all right, he was told, he'd be compensated.

The constable returned with Jason. He'd not seen any sign of a girl anywhere along the road.

'Told you she was a liar, didn't I?' said Lenny. 'Can't believe a bleeding word she says.'

I would have pushed his horrible face in if I'd had the chance. I felt quite violent towards him, more than I ever had towards anyone in my life.

The air had cooled and I was chilly in my T-shirt without a jacket. Time was moving on and still the detectives were busy. My left hand was free, so I was able to lift it and take a look at my watch. Twenty past seven! My parents would be phoning Charlotte. *Have you seen Emily this afternoon?*

It was another half-hour before the detectives finally emerged from the van. They had a good haul. They spread it out on the grass in front of Lenny and asked him to look at it.

'It was found in the van you've been living in. Have you any comment to make?'

'Never seen any of it. Must have been put there before we took the van. Previous tenants could have had it stashed in there.'

The policeman turned to me. 'Would you take a look, please?'

'I've never seen any of it either,' I said. 'I don't even know what the stuff is.'

'Take a guess.'

'Well, drugs, I suppose.'

'You suppose right.'

'You see, she's not as innocent as she seems,' said Lenny.

They locked the van door and told the manager he was not to touch anything. Then Lenny and I – the two suspects! – were shepherded down through the park to the road where three police vehicles were lined up. Lenny protested all the way. I kept quiet. I was told to get into the back of one of the cars and my attached policewoman slid in beside me. A detective took the wheel and we set off into town.

I kept my head down. I knew too many people in the city. What would they think if they saw me riding in the back of a *police* car? It would be just like Mr or Mrs McDowell to be standing on a corner. I was relieved when we reached the police station and went inside. It wouldn't take long, surely not, to sort out this ghastly mistake.

I was taken into an interview room where I was asked my particulars.

'You still maintain that your name is Emily Malone?'

'Yes.'

'Have you ever been known as Eve?'

'No, never.'

'Mr Smith seemed to know you as that.'

'He'd lie about anything!'

'And the manager at the caravan site.'

'He's mistaken. You see, we look alike, Eve and I. Anyone who didn't know us very well might confuse us.'

'Would you say Mr Smith knew you well?'

'He knew *Eve* well. But I'm not her.'

Did they believe me? I couldn't tell. Their faces were blank.

'And you say that this is your address?' They read it out to me.

I confirmed it. I told them that my father's name was John and my mother's Mary. I added, 'She's a lawyer.' I didn't know whether that would help me or not. They might not be too fond of lawyers.

'Are they aware that you have been visiting this caravan site?'

I shook my head. They said they'd send someone round to ask my parents – if that was what they were! – to come to the station.

I was taken to a cell and given a cup of tea, then the policewoman left and locked the door on the other side. The whole world had gone screwy around me. Here was I, a *prisoner*, suspected of being in possession of drugs! I drank the cup of tea, for my throat was parched, but after I'd drained the mug I couldn't sit still. I paced up and down the small strip of floor, in the way I suppose that prisoners often do. What if my parents had gone out? I might be here for hours. How long could they hold me? Should I ask to see a lawyer if my mother didn't come?

But she came, half an hour later, accompanied by the policewoman.

'Emily!' she cried. 'What's been happening to you?'

'Oh, Mum!' I went into her arms and then the tears came.

When I'd dried my eyes my mother said, 'Come on, let's sit down and you can tell me everything.'

Everything? I couldn't do that without involving my father. If I had to tell my mother the whole truth I didn't want the policewoman listening in to the private details of our family's life. She was standing by the door with her arms folded and evidently intended to stay.

'Where's Dad?' I asked.

'Working late.'

'So he doesn't know yet?'

'I left him a note on the kitchen table. Now then, you must tell me how you came to be mixed up in all this.'

'I don't know where to start. It's a bit of a muddle.'

'It's to do with a caravan, isn't it? Let's begin with that. And a young man called Lenny Smith. Is he the one you met yesterday?'

With everything else that had been going on, I'd clean forgotten Greg. I should have met him at a quarter to eight on the bridge at Stockbridge. He wouldn't be there now, he wouldn't have waited that long. It was gone nine. He'd think I'd stood him up.

'No, it's not him,' I said miserably.

'So how did you come to go there?'

'Well, you see, I met this girl called Eve –'

'Where?'

'Can't remember exactly. I saw her around, in charity shops and so forth. We got talking.'

'Did she engage you in conversation first?'

'Yes.'

'And then what?'

'Well, she was living at this caravan with Lenny.'

'She invited you out there?'

'She took me out. But then when I went today she wasn't there.'

'So you went more than once? How many times did you go?'

'Three.' That made my mother frown. She was beginning to think I was in deeper than she had imagined.

'So she wasn't there?'

'No. He was.'

'On his own? But you went in?' Her frown was deepening. 'Why?'

'To wait for Eve.' This was as bad as being interrogated by the police, perhaps worse, for I didn't know at which point I was going to give everything away. I continued hurriedly, 'Then the police came and raided the van and they thought I was her.'

'I think they've accepted now that you are not this girl Eve. I brought your passport with me. Did they find anything in the van?'

'Drugs. Quite a lot.'

'I see.' My mother sat back. 'So you were actually on the premises when the drugs were found?'

'But they can't charge me, can they?' I asked anxiously. 'Surely they can't?'

Before she could answer the door opened and one of the male constables who'd been on the raid came in. 'We're letting you go,' he said.

I was stunned. One moment I was feeling caught in a tangled web, the next I was told that I could go, that I was free!

'You're not charging her?' asked my mother.

'No. We've got the real Eve out there. She was picked up half an hour ago.' He looked at me. 'She told us you had nothing to do with it.'

I couldn't speak, I was too exhausted.

'If we go ahead and charge Mr Smith we may wish to bring you in again to make a statement.'

'That will be fine,' said my mother. 'You know where to find us. Let's get you home then, Emily.' She put her hand under my elbow and helped me up.

We followed the policeman out of the cell and along the corridor to the entrance lobby. Eve was standing there flanked by the two plain-clothes detectives. I drew in my breath. When my mother saw her would she suspect?

At that moment, the outside door swung open and in came my father with the air of someone who has been hurrying. He saw Eve first and a look of consternation crossed his face.

Then he saw my mother and me.

Chapter 15

My father looked from Eve to me and then helplessly at my mother.

It was up to my mother to assume the lead. 'I'm about to take Emily home,' she said. 'It was a case of mistaken identity.'

'It's me they want,' said Eve.

'But the drugs belonged to Lenny,' I cried. 'You didn't want him to have them. They can't pin it on you.'

'It seems you know more about these drugs than you were letting on,' said the policewoman. She went to consult with the detectives. My mother gave me a look that told me it would have been better if I'd kept my mouth shut. But I couldn't have. Eve had helped me to get off the hook so I'd had to help her.

My father said in a quiet, strangled sort of voice, 'There are a lot of things I have to tell you, Mary, that I've been meaning to tell you. But it was difficult, very difficult, and somehow or other . . .' He shook his head.

'This is hardly the place.' Even then she could not have guessed his secret.

One of the detectives came over to me and said they would like me to make a statement before going home since it seemed, after all, that I did have some knowledge of the drugs. My mother could accompany me.

'I'll go with Eve,' said my father.

Now my mother did look startled, but the detective was waiting to escort us to the interview room so she had no chance to question my father. I gave Eve one last glance. She raised a hand to me.

I made my statement and then we were told we could leave. There was no sign of either Eve or my father in the entrance lobby. My mother went up to the desk sergeant and asked if Mr Malone had gone home.

'Not yet, madam. He's in the interview room with his daughter.'

'But this is his daughter. It was me who was in the interview room with –' My mother's voice faded.

We didn't speak on the way home. My mother drove as efficiently and smoothly as ever and managed to manoeuvre the car into a small parking space in the street. We went into the house.

'I think a cup of tea might be in order,' she said, going ahead of me into the kitchen. 'And you must be needing some food.'

She made a pot of tea and put bread in the toaster and set out butter and cheese and some cooked ham. I sat slumped at the table.

'Try to eat something,' she urged. 'Your blood sugar will be way down.'

I made an effort and managed a few bites and drank a cup of tea. My mother poured herself a whisky and sat down. It was unlike her to drink whisky late at night. She seldom drank it at all.

'Do you know about all this, Emily?'

Reluctantly I nodded. 'But I think Dad should tell you.'

'You're right, he should. It's not up to you to do it. And now I think you should go on up to bed.'

I kissed my mother goodnight and gave her an extra hug and then I went up to my room. Tired though I was, I knew I would not be able to sleep until I'd found out what was happening to Eve. I heard Mum coming up the stairs after me and going into the drawing room, which was next to my room. She put on some music, with the volume turned down low.

I waited by the window, watching the street. It was fully parked up by now; Dad would have to leave the car a street or two away, so he would arrive on foot. The minutes ticked by. Midnight came and went. No one came and went along the street. Most of the houses were dark. Perhaps my father would not come back at all.

At five minutes past one I heard footsteps on the pavement. It was him. I fled out of the room and down the stairs, not turning back when my mother called after me, 'Emily, where are you going?' I met my father at the gate. He let me come into his arms and I felt sure he was crying. I was. 'I'm sorry, love, I really am,' he kept on saying. 'You didn't deserve this.'

'I love you, Dad,' I said.

'And I love you, Emily. And your mother. But is she going to believe that?'

'I don't know. But tell me about Eve. What happened?'

'They released her, without charge. It's Mr Smith, alias fifty other names, that they want. The Essex police had been looking for him under one of them for a number of offences, including grievous bodily harm, and absconding with an under-age girl.'

'But where is Eve?' I cried. 'She didn't go back to the caravan?'

'No, I took her to your Aunt Etta's. And now we'd better go in.'

I kept my arm through his but as we approached the door I let it drop. I didn't want my mother to think I was taking his side against her and I think he understood that.

'Thank you, Emily,' he murmured.

My mother was waiting in the hall. I went to bed without another word, leaving them to sort it out, if they could.

I slept at once and woke to find it was eleven o'clock in the morning. I jumped up and went down to the kitchen in my dressing gown to find my mother seated at the kitchen table drinking tea. She poured me a cup and I sat down.

'I let you sleep in. I didn't think you'd want to go to school today.'

I didn't think I'd want to go back to school ever. 'Are you not going to work, either?'

'No, not today.'

'Where's Dad?' I asked fearfully, looking round as if he might be lurking in the larder.

'He's decided to move out for a little while. I need some space around me at the moment, Emily, to try to come to terms with everything. I expect you understand that?'

'Where's he gone?'

'He has a flat empty near his office. The tenants have just moved out.'

I was afraid he might have gone to Aunt Etta's, to join Eve, and form a new family.

I didn't dare ask my mother how she felt about Dad's affair. She's a very private person and doesn't show her feelings easily, unlike Dad. It must have been hard for him to keep his secret buttoned up inside him all these years, except of course that he did have his sister to talk to. I found it easier to be with him when something emotional was happening in the house for I knew where I was with him and what he was thinking. But I was aware that there was no point in blaming my mother for being as she was. Her way was just different. It was he himself who'd made that point to me.

'I think I'll have a shower and go out for a bit.' I got up.

'Emily –' My mother hesitated. 'I would rather you didn't try to see the girl again.'

'But, Mum!' It had been my intention to see her. 'Why shouldn't I?'

'Well, she does spell trouble, doesn't she? And perhaps we have enough to be going on with.'

'But that's not her fault!'

'I know, essentially it's your father's. Otherwise she wouldn't be here at all. And I can't blame her for wanting to see him but you, you're a different matter.'

'She's my half-sister. Doesn't that mean anything?'

'I doubt if she was overly concerned with your welfare, taking you out to that caravan, knowing there were drugs in it. And then there was that man who was wanted by the police, with a record. She has a record too. Didn't she tell you that?'

I sat down again.

'For being in possession of drugs. Truanting from school. Theft. Your father said she's been in various young offenders' institutions.'

'But she's had a terrible life. No wonder she's been in trouble! What with her mother dying –'

'Her mother isn't dead. Your father spoke to her two days ago, to let her know where the girl was. She'd notified the police that she was missing.'

'I don't believe it!'

'I'm afraid it's true. You have to accept the fact that not everything she told you might be true.'

'I'm going to go and ask her.' I made for the door.

'It would be better for you to take a step back, Emily. But the decision is yours.'

I was now in a state of indecision. I was no longer in a rebellious mood to go clean against my mother's wishes but, on the other hand, she had said it was my decision. And therefore, by implication, my responsibility. I felt willing to take that on. I showered and dressed and took out my bike. I cycled slowly down to Leith, trying to get used to the idea that Eve had lied to me. But the central fact remained true: that she was related to me by blood. We were sisters. And I did want to see her again.

I turned into the street where Aunt Etta lived. For a moment I hesitated, then I put my finger on the bell and waited, my ear close to the grille, my hand on the door ready to push it when I heard her voice. No sound emerged. I pressed again, holding for a longer time. I tried four times in all. I decided they must have gone out, perhaps to shop or get some air. It was a nice day, mild, with intermittent sunshine. I went in pursuit of them, round the highways and byways of Leith and came across my father who was sitting on a wall looking out over the water. I sat down beside him.

'I've been round at Aunt Etta's,' I said.

'They've gone.'

'*Gone?* Where?'

'I put them on the half-past-eleven train to London.'

'Oh no! I've missed her then.'

'She had to go back. Her mother is meeting them at the other end.'

'You know, I thought she was dead.' Another possibility had entered my head: now that Eve's mother was still alive Dad might want to go to her. 'Were you very much in love with her?'

'It's difficult to know, really, it was so long ago. It was a spell of madness, your mother and I had been having problems, our marriage was going through a rocky patch.' He shrugged. 'I'm not trying to make excuses for myself.'

'But it was quite a long spell of madness. It went on for a couple of years, didn't it?'

'A couple of years? No, only for two weekends.'

'But Eve said –' I stopped.

We sat in silence side by side watching the seagulls wheeling over the water.

Chapter 16

Eve had said a lot of things which I now had to reconsider in a different light. The central part of what she had told me was true, that she was the child of a relationship between my father and her mother, but she had embellished it, blown it up, in an effort to turn it into a romantic love story. She had told it as she would have liked it to have been.

'Dad, OK, so she's a liar and a number of other things as well, but I can't really believe she's all bad.'

'No, I'm sure she's not. I guess she got off on the wrong foot at some point. Maybe it was because of me. Or rather the absence of me.'

Not everyone without a father went off the rails, I pointed out. 'You grew up without a dad.'

'I had Etta. And my mother was a strong woman, who wouldn't let herself go to the wall no matter what life threw at her. Joyce, Eve's mother, started to drink. She lost her job. So it's not been easy for Eve.' My father stood up. 'Let's walk,' he said.

We covered miles of the city that day and as we walked we talked. He wanted to do something for Eve, to try to help her get on to an even keel. He thought she was intelligent, and so did I, and that she should go back to school and finish her education. We discussed the best way to go about it and he came to the conclusion that Eve and her mother first had to be helped to move out of the place they were in – an estate ridden with drugs and other crimes – to accommodation in a new area. It would give Eve a fresh start, a chance to change direction. It would be up to her then to take it or not. Neither of us could predict if she would. Dad said he would buy a small flat for her and her mother and pay a monthly allowance towards Eve's upkeep until she had finished her education.

'That's about all I can do.'

'Will you go to see her?'

'Yes, I think I will, from time to time.'

We parted and I went home to my mother. She was very quiet and she asked me no questions. I volunteered the information that I had not seen Eve, that she had left town. My mother merely nodded and did not ask how I knew. I dare say she guessed that I had seen my father. Was she going to be able to forgive him? That I could not guess.

When Ben phoned that evening, before calling my mother, I said to him, 'Momentous things have been happening around here. I wish you could come home. I can't tell you anything on the phone and don't say anything when you speak to Mum. She and Dad have separated temporarily.'

'*Separated?* Where is Dad?'

'Is it Ben?' my mother asked, coming into the hall.

I surrendered the phone. I left the kitchen door ajar so that I was able to catch part of their conversation.

'You'll have to ask your father,' she said. 'I'd rather he told you.'

Charlotte was next to phone. Charlotte! My best friend. I had almost forgotten about her. She wanted to know how ill I really was and if I would be coming back to school next day. I said I thought not. I didn't want to go back and take my place there until I knew what was going to happen between my parents. The following day was Friday.

'I might be back on Monday.'

'How about Lover Boy? Mr Dream Boat. What was his name again? Greg?'

I had not forgotten about Greg, I had pushed him back into the recesses of my mind until I would have time to think about him properly.

'How did you get on? Last night?'

'I wasn't able to go.'

'Oh no! What a disappointment! Have you got another date lined up?'

'Not yet.'

'Is he going to phone you?'

'Probably.'

'But not *definitely*?' She was intrigued.

'Charlotte, I must go. Mum wants the phone.'

When I put down the receiver I now had Greg lodged in the forefront of my mind. I still hoped he would phone, that he might think something unforeseen had stopped me coming and that I had not just stood him up. But he didn't phone that evening. I had a restless night and when I slept I had a jumbled dream in which my father and mother and Eve and a man who looked like Greg but yet did not seem to be him kept appearing and reappearing like shaken pieces in a kaleidoscope.

In the morning my mother suggested I might be better going back to school, but I couldn't face it. I didn't want Charlotte cross-questioning me. Like her mother, she has a nose for gossip. For a start, she would wonder why my father wasn't driving us to school. My mother understood, so didn't press me and went off to work herself.

I decided I would have to try to track Greg down. The only thing I knew about him, apart from the fact that he was a motor mechanic, was that he lived in a flat at Tollcross. I didn't even know his surname, so I couldn't try looking him up in the phone book. I waited until afternoon, then went up to Tollcross and hung about, hoping for inspiration. He would be at work, but if I stayed around for a few hours I might meet him coming home.

Tollcross is part of the inner city. It's a busy intersection where several lanes of traffic converge and spiral off in different directions. Here you can find cafes, restaurants, bars and grocers, a cinema, a theatre, chemists and shops selling carpets, designer kitchens, computers and fish and chips amongst numerous other things. There is also an information centre, a post office, a couple of banks and an amusement arcade. Almost everything you could possibly need, in fact. There isn't a single rose bush to be seen, or any trees with branches overhanging the pavement.

Above the shops are flats, about a century old, built of stone, tenement style. Modern blocks stand on two corner sites where previous buildings have been demolished. Greg must live in one of the older flats, I deduced, since he'd said he'd lived there since he was a boy. I wandered up and down, vaguely reading names over doorbells, even though I was aware that would get me nowhere. I went into a cafe and bought a coffee. The waitress was young, not much older than me. When she was wiping down the table next to mine I got into conversation with her. I asked her if she'd been working here long and she said six weeks.

'Do you like it?'

She shrugged. Maybe it was a silly question.

'Do you get a lot of regulars?'

'One or two. Old man comes in every morning for a cup of tea, sits here half the day reading his racing paper.'

That didn't sound too promising. 'You wouldn't know a guy called Greg, would you?'

'Greg?' She frowned.

'No, I don't suppose you would. He lives round here. Tall, good looking, brown eyes?'

'Wouldn't mind knowing somebody like that!' Someone was trying to attract her attention. She moved off to serve them. I returned to the streets.

The big clock in the middle of the intersection said four twenty. I reckoned that he might come home any time between now and six o'clock. I patrolled the four arms of the streets that cross there, going a short distance along each, keeping the clock in sight as far as I could, looking back every few steps, turning in circles, trying to have eyes everywhere. I thought I saw him at one point, going into Boots the chemist. I ran like mad along the pavement, dodging pedestrians who gave me dirty looks, but when I reached the shop and went inside and scouted up and down the aisles I saw that I'd been mistaken. The boy who was standing in front of the rack of toothbrushes and whom I'd thought was Greg did not look remotely like him. Would I recognise him? I was beginning to wonder if I would.

When the hands of the clock crept round to six thirty I had to give up. I felt deflated and exhausted and my eyes ached from peering into the distance.

I stayed at home all evening in case he would phone. As the minutes and then the hours passed I became resigned to the idea that he would not. And he didn't.

Ben came home next day. He had hitched, which earned him a reprimand from our mother, but she was pleased to see him nevertheless.

'Did the play fold?' she asked.

'No, I came home because, well, it seems we're in the middle of a family crisis?'

'We are, rather.' She gave a faint smile. 'Maybe Emily will fill you in on the basic details, Ben. I'm going out to meet your father.'

And with that our mother left us. Was it a good sign that they were having a meeting? We would have to wait to find out.

Ben was bowled over of course when he heard about Eve and it took him some time to take it all in. 'Poor Dad,' he said, shaking his head. 'And poor Mum.'

'Let's go out. I can't bear to hang about waiting to hear.'

We walked up to Princes Street, which was heaving with shoppers and crossed over to the gardens. It was a fine day and people were out and about strolling along the paths, lying on the grass, picnicking. We bought ice creams and ate them as we walked. We took a quieter path underneath the castle rock and found a spot to sit down. I was engrossed in my ice cream when I glanced up and saw Greg approaching. He was with a girl.

I didn't know what to do. I sat there, frozen, the ice cream halfway to my mouth, as if I were playing the game of statues. They came closer and soon would draw level with us. As they did I looked straight up into his face and he looked down into mine. We recognised each other. I saw his eyes flicker briefly over Ben and perhaps mine flickered momentarily over the girl at his side. He did not speak. Neither did I. And then they had passed us by and were heading back up towards Princes Street.

'Who was that?' asked Ben.

'A boy I met.' I told him about Greg.

'You should have spoken to him.'

'How could I? When he was with another girl. He didn't speak to me, did he?'

'He saw you were with me. He wouldn't have known I was your brother.'

I stood up straining to see them, but they had got lost in the crowd.

'She might have been his sister,' said Ben.

'She didn't look like him, did she? She had blonde hair.'

'I don't look like you.'

I was tormented by the thought that she might have been his sister and, if so, that I had let the opportunity slip, but I was also tormented by the thought that he had found another girl and it hadn't taken him long. Maybe he picked up girls on buses every day of the week.

'Bit risky, mind you,' said Ben, 'picking up men on buses!'

'I don't *usually* do that.'

'I should hope not. Another time let me vet him first.'

'You're not always around, are you?' I wished he were. I was so pleased he was home and I had someone I could talk to openly.

'There'll be someone else soon,' predicted Ben, but I wasn't so sure. I didn't think I'd be able to shift Greg out of my mind that easily.

When Mum came back she told us calmly and quietly that our father would be returning the next day. Neither Ben nor I gave a shout of jubilation for we both knew she would not have welcomed that.

'We're going to try to rebuild. We came to the conclusion that what we had was too valuable to throw away.'

'Good,' said Ben. 'I'm glad.'

She came and stood between us and put an arm round each of our shoulders.

So Dad came back the next day and for a while the atmosphere in the house was subdued, but soon it took on its ordinary tempo again, almost as if nothing had happened to disturb it, though not quite. We were not as relaxed with one another as we used to be. Eve, though not physically present in our house, had cast a shadow over us. It didn't mean we couldn't function as a family. It was more a feeling that part of the sun had been blotted out. That was how Ben put it.

He left a few days later, and after he'd gone I had another of my restless spells. Situation normal, I was beginning to think. I went out on my own for long walks round the city. I wasn't actively seeking Greg, I'd decided that wouldn't do any good – you know how it is when you look too hard for something, you never find it, so it's better to leave it alone and wait. And there was the possibility that the blonde girl might not have been his sister. That was a factor I couldn't ignore. Perhaps the time hadn't been right for us.

I have the feeling, an irrational gut feeling, perhaps, that we will run across each other again one of these days. And then, if we are still attracted, we might take up where we left off, and it might not be quite as crazy as it was on that first and only date I had with him. A lot has happened to me since then. I've changed. Charlotte keeps telling me I have. She says it in an accusing tone of voice and in response I can only shrug. So at times she's fed up with me, especially when I won't go out in a foursome with Mark and Donald. But we'll remain friends, I know that, even if there has been a shift in our relationship. I have come to see that relationships can cope with shifts and still work. They just need a bit of time to resettle. I only have to look at my parents to know that.

And then there's Eve. She haunts my dreams as well as my imagination. I have the feeling that I will see her again too. I *must* see her. We were cut off from each other too soon. There are so many things I want to say to her, to ask her. One day, when I am wandering idly along by the shops in Stockbridge, she'll emerge from the shadows. I'll stop and she'll raise a hand to acknowledge me. Sometimes I think that I do see her, but when I blink and look again I realise that the pavement is empty. But I'm confident that the day will come when she will be there in the flesh and not as a figment of my imagination. I will cross the road and we will meet and start to walk, and to talk, and perhaps even to fall out, and fall in again. Just like sisters.

Me and my shadow, we'll stroll down the avenue . . . together.

ALSO IN

Heinemann
New Windmills

Founding Editors: Anne and Ian Serraillier

Chinua Achebe Things Fall Apart
David Almond Skellig
Maya Angelou I Know Why the Caged Bird Sings
Margaret Atwood The Handmaid's Tale
Jane Austen Pride and Prejudice
Stan Barstow Joby: A Kind of Loving
Nina Bawden Carrie's War; The Finding; Humbug
Malorie Blackman Tell Me No Lies; Words Last Forever
Charlotte Brontë Jane Eyre
Emily Brontë Wuthering Heights
Melvin Burgess and Lee Hall Billy Elliot
Betsy Byars The Midnight Fox; The Pinballs; The Eighteenth Emergency
Victor Canning The Runaways
Sir Arthur Conan Doyle Sherlock Holmes Short Stories
Susan Cooper King of Shadows
Robert Cormier Heroes
Roald Dahl Danny; The Champion of the World; The Wonderful
Story of Henry Sugar; George's Marvellous Medicine; The Witches;
Boy; Going Solo; Matilda; My Year
Anita Desai The Village by the Sea
Charles Dickens A Christmas Carol; Great Expectations; A Charles
Dickens Selection
Berlie Doherty Granny was a Buffer Girl; Street Child
Roddy Doyle Paddy Clarke Ha Ha Ha
George Eliot Silas Marner
Anne Fine The Granny Project
Leon Garfield Six Shakespeare Stories
Ann Halam Dr Franklin's Island
Thomas Hardy The Withered Arm and Other Wessex Tales; The Mayor
of Casterbridge
Ernest Hemmingway The Old Man and the Sea; A Farewell to Arms
Barry Hines A Kestrel For A Knave
Nigel Hinton Buddy; Buddy's Song
Anne Holm I Am David

Janni Howker Badger on the Barge; The Nature of the Beast;
Martin Farrell
Pete Johnson The Protectors
Geraldine Kaye Comfort Herself
Daniel Keyes Flowers for Algernon
Dick King-Smith The Sheep-Pig
Elizabeth Laird Red Sky in the Morning
D H Lawrence The Fox and The Virgin and the Gypsy; Selected Tales
Harper Lee To Kill a Mockingbird
C Day Lewis The Otterbury Incident
Joan Linguard Across the Barricades
Penelope Lively The Ghost of Thomas Kemp
Geraldine McCaughrean Stories from Shakespeare; Pack of Lies
Bernard MacLaverty Cal; The Best of Bernard MacLaverty
Jan Mark Heathrow Nights
James Vance Marshall Walkabout
Ian McEwan The Daydreamer; A Child in Time
Michael Morpurgo The Wreck of the Zanzibar; Why the Whales Came;
Arthur, High King of Britain; Kensuke's Kingdom; From Hereabout Hill;
Robin of Sherwood
Beverley Naidoo No Turning Back; The Other Side of Truth
Bill Naughton The Goalkeeper's Revenge
New Windmill A Charles Dickens Selection
New Windmill Anthology of Challenging Texts: Thoughtlines
New Windmill Book of Classic Short Stories
New Windmill Book of Fiction and Non-fiction: Taking Off!
New Windmill Book of Greek Myths
New Windmill Book of Haunting Tales
New Windmill Book of Humorous Stories: Don't Make Me Laugh
New Windmill Book of Nineteenth Century Short Stories
New Windmill Book of Non-fiction: Get Real
New Windmill Book of Non-fiction: Real Lives, Real Times
New Windmill Book of Scottish Short Stories
New Windmill Book of Short Stories: Fast and Curious
New Windmill Book of Short Stories: From Beginning to End
New Windmill Book of Short Stories: Into the Unknown
New Windmill Book of Short Stories: Tales with a Twist
New Windmill Book of Short Stories: Trouble in Two Centuries
New Windmill Book of Short Stories: Ways with Words
New Windmill Book of Stories from Many Cultures and Traditions;
Fifty-Fifty Tuti-Fruity Chocolate Chip

How many have you read?